G000060475

Come What MAY

LK FARLOW

© 2020 by LK Farlow

All rights reserved.
Cover Design: Y'all. That Graphic.

Interior Formatting: Serendipity Formatting
Editing: Librum Artis Editorial Services & My Brother's Editor
Proofreading: Deaton Author Services

No part of this publication may be reproduced, distributed, or
transmitted in any form or by any means, including photocopying,
recording, or other electronic or mechanical methods, without the prior
written permission of the author, except in the case of brief quotations
in a book review.

This is a work of fiction. Names, characters, businesses, places, events
and incidents are either the products of the author's imagination or used
in a fictitious manner. Any resemblance to actual persons, living or dead,
or actual events is purely coincidental.

The author acknowledges the trademark status and trademark owners
of various products referred to in this work of fiction, which have been
used without permission. The publication/use of these trademarks is not
authorized, associated with, or sponsored by the trademark owners.

www.authorlkfarlow.com

To my Phoobs, for always being here for me,
come what may.

SERAPHINE

I CRUMPLE THE NOTE FOR THE HUNDREDTH TIME. I DON'T know why I'm clutching it like a lifeline—I have the stupid thing memorized. The words are etched into my heart at this point, each sloppily scrawled letter pumping through my veins like the worst kind of poison.

He said he loved me. Over and over, he said that. And not to blame myself… that his choice was as much for me as it was him. But how? Actions over words, and at the end of it all, he left me. *By choice.*

Deep down—like marrow deep—I know I'm being unfair. But life's not fair, and now, I'm alone. Completely and totally alone.

Tears fall freely, running unchecked down my cheeks as the minister drones on about the wonders of life after death. Which is bullshit, because there's no wonder for those of us the dead leave behind, just a whole lot of fucking heartache.

"You okay?" My cousin's whispered concern jars me.

I shake my head in lieu of an actual reply. I'm pretty

sure I'm not capable of more than gut-wrenching sobs right now.

"Sweet girl." She clasps my hand in hers, and while I want to pull away, I let her hold on to me, knowing she needs the comfort, too. He left us both, after all. "Do you want to stay with us tonight?"

I'm tempted to take her up on the offer—the thought of being alone in the house we shared is honestly crippling. But Magnolia and Simon don't need me intruding, so again, I shake my head.

"It's not good for you to be alone," she says, tightening her grip on my hand.

Alone. The word fills me with bitterness, coating my insides with an inky darkness as it wraps around my heart.

"I'm fine." I force my lips up into what I hope is a smile. "Promise."

Magnolia sighs. "If you say so."

"I do."

She sighs again, and we both tune back in just in time to hear the minister ask me to come to the podium to say a few words. I don't know what I was thinking when I agreed to this. Clearly, I wasn't—because I'd rather eat glass than go up to the pulpit and tell all these people who didn't give a single shit about my father while he was living how great he was. Because if they'd have spent even five minutes with him, they'd already know.

Sure, there's a handful of people here who truly loved him—but these fools probably couldn't tell you a single authentic thing about him. Yet they have the audacity to sniffle and cry into their tissues.

I shove my growing ire down as I make my way to the

front. My knees wobble as I step onto the raised platform. On a shuddering exhale, I turn and face the crowd. "Y'all knew him as Dave, but to me, he was Dad. Those three letters were more than a title, more than a name. To him, it was a badge of honor."

A tear-soaked laugh slips past my lips as I struggle to maintain my composure. "His two favorite things to talk about were cars and—" I slap a hand over my mouth as a sob overtakes my words. My shoulders shake as my grief barrels into me like a runaway train.

After a few moments, I wipe my eyes and continue, keeping my eyes cast downward—the last thing I need right now is to *see* any of these people feeling sorry for me.

"And me. He… he left us before his time, and in his illness, he left a lot of things unfinished, but through it all, he never once allowed me to question his love for me. Even when he was bedridden and too weak to talk, he'd hold my hand and I could just… *feel*… his love."

I swallow hard and finally dare to look up. A shiver runs through me when my eyes lock with those of Mateo Reyes. His stare is intense and sorrowful all at once, and for reasons unknown, it makes me feel a little more at peace.

"Dad had a kind word for everyone, and he'd give you the shirt off his back. He believed in honesty and hard work. He was a blue-collar man, through and through. He is—*was*—" I shrug and sniffle at the same time, existing in that weird space between laughter and tears. "A good man. The kind who put others first and believed time was more valuable than money."

As I near the end of my poorly planned speech, self-doubt creeps in uninvited and smothers any bit of confidence I was feeling. *God, these people probably think I'm a blathering idiot.*

Swiping angrily at my tear-stained cheeks, I power on, ignoring what feels like an elephant sitting on my chest. "He always said, 'It's what you do while you're alive that matters.' Honor him—" My voice breaks and my breath saws in and out of my lungs. I'm milliseconds from losing it. "Honor him by making the most of each and every day."

I rush down from the platform, forgoing the steps altogether in my haste to escape. With tears streaming, I race down the aisle and through the parlor doors into the parking lot. The service isn't finished, but I can't bear to spend another second inside of the chapel.

The humidity outside is thick, as if the loss coating my insides is so great that even the air feels weighted with it. I wrap my arms tightly around my middle as I suck in a greedy lungful of air, trying with all my might to exhale even a fraction of my pain.

It's no use, though.

My cries turn to heaving sobs as I break down in the middle of the funeral home parking lot, for God and everyone who might happen by to see. Uncaring of the show I may be putting on, I purge myself of the anger, sadness, uncertainty, and fear until all that's left is a heaping pile of sorrowful resentment.

I'm so caught up in my grief that when a strong hand comes down on my shoulder, I nearly fall over.

"Seraphine."

Mateo Reyes.

As it always has, the way my name rolls off of his

tongue sends a little jolt of inappropriate excitement through me. As a friend of my father and sixteen years my senior, he's well off-limits. Regardless, my heart never got the memo and always beats a little harder anytime he's near.

"Turn around." The barest amount of pressure to my shoulder accompanies the command, and I pivot to face him, inwardly cringing at the picture I must paint after breaking down so thoroughly.

I try to keep my eyes low, but Mateo's not having it. "Look at me," he says, skimming the knuckle of his index finger down the line of my jaw to lift my gaze to his. "Keep your chin up, *mariposita*. He wouldn't like to see your tears."

"Then maybe he should be here." I sound like a little snot, but I can't bring myself to care. Because I mean it—if my dad didn't want my tears, maybe he shouldn't have killed himself.

He gives me a long look, his deep chocolate eyes twinkling with the kind of knowledge that only comes with experience and age. "Death hurts. Like a motherfucker. You can either let the pain cripple you or you can own it." He skims his knuckles back up my jaw and whispers, "*Te esperan dias mejores*." He drags his eyes over me once more before abruptly turning and walking away.

My eyes stay glued to him as he retreats back into the funeral home, all the while wondering what made him come after me and what the hell he just said.

The morning after Dad's funeral dawns bright and sunny. The birds are chirping, and there's not a cloud in the sky. The temperature is perfectly mild, and there's a nice breeze in the air.

It's the perfect fall day, and it makes me want to rage. To kick, scream, and cry. To destroy all of the good and pretty things, to raze it all to the ground until nothing but charred ash remains.

I want the earth around me to match my pain, not to torment me with its beauty. I want the sky to weep right along with me.

However, the universe does not share my grief, and while I'm a little self-destructive, I have no plans to destroy anything other than Dad's leftover beer in the fridge.

My cell rings right as I pop the top on the can. "Hey, Myles," I say before gulping back a sip.

"Hey, girl. How are you?"

I take another healthy swallow before replying. "Tired. Sad. Angry. All of the above." I should probably try to be a little more professional, but I'm hoping she's calling as a friend right now, instead of as my boss. And if not, here's to hoping she'll give me a little grace, under the circumstances.

"I'm truly sorry for your loss, Seraphine. Your daddy was a good man, and those who knew him will miss him thoroughly."

"Yeah." I croak out the single word as my sadness lodges in my throat.

"Anyway, I was calling to tell you, if you need to take some time off, we understand."

"No!" I spit the word out in a panic. The thought of

sitting here, staring at our home without him in it, is too much to bear. "I'll be there Tuesday when we open."

"Are you sure?"

I chug back the rest of the can and open another. "Mmhmm," I mumble around a mouthful of the hoppy liquid.

"Okay. Well, I'll see you Tuesday then." She sounds unsure, but luckily, she doesn't call me on it. Probably because, like me, she was raised by a single parent, too. In her case, it was her grandmother after her mama abandoned her. Either way, I'm thankful she doesn't question me.

"Yup, see you then."

The rest of my day is spent on the couch, drinking Dad's beer, watching mindless television until I fall into a restless sleep.

Monday was spent in much the same way—drinking, crying, napping, and all-around avoiding doing anything important. Like dealing with Dad's shop or figuring out the bills or his life insurance—though, I'm sure with him taking his own life, that's a moot point.

At one point, someone knocked on the door, but I didn't bother checking to see who. The one person I want to see is no longer here.

Now, it's Tuesday, and that storm I wanted a few days ago is here.

Rain falls from the sky in sheets as lightning flashes wickedly through the dark clouds. It's perfect, really, because the storm can totally explain not only why I'm an hour late, but also why I look like crap.

It's a win-win, really. Mostly. Though these wet shoes can go right to hell, along with my headache.

I push open the door to Southern Roots—the salon I'm apprenticing at—and promptly slip, landing hard on my bottom. "Shit!" I moan, making no move to pull myself back up.

"Seraphine!" Myla Rose rushes over to me, her mom-mode activated. "Are you okay?"

"Peachy," I mumble as she helps me back to my feet.

"Have you been sleeping?" Azalea, Myla Rose's business partner, asks from the stool behind the desk. *Jesus, I didn't even notice her.*

A shoulder shrug is my only reply.

"Are you sure you're up for working right now?" Myla asks. "You were over an hour late, and if you need some time—"

"It's the rain. Cats and dogs. It made me late."

"Forget about sleeping," Azalea says, rounding the desk. "Have you been drinking?"

"No!"

"Liar!" Azalea leans in and sniffs me. "You reek of alcohol. Are you freaking drunk?"

"Fine, yes."

Myla Rose takes my hand in hers and squeezes gently. Something about her soft touch has me tearing up and before I know it, I'm a snotty, sniffling mess, blubbering like a madwoman in front of the entire salon.

"What's going on?" Magnolia asks from somewhere deeper in the salon. "Oh, Seraphine." She comes to my other side and pulls me into her arms.

Azalea watches us for a moment before speaking up. "I don't mean to sound like an insensitive bitch, but, S, maybe you should take some time off."

It's on the tip of my tongue to refuse, to demand she allow me to stay and work, but I don't. I know she's right. I'm a mess right now—and a poor representation of the salon she and Myla Rose have worked so hard to build. I won't let their hard work be consumed by the black hole that is my grief.

"Yeah, okay."

The three women—my only real friends, even if they are older and my co-workers-slash-employers—fall into conversation, talking about me as though I'm not here. Making plans and such. It's a blur really, until Myla Rose addresses me directly.

"Cash is on his way here. I'm gonna drive you home, and he's gonna follow in your car. You're in no state to drive. We will figure out your apprenticeship hours later, and I'll handle moving any appointments you may have had, and the three of us will split your other duties. We love you and want the best for you, you know that, right?"

I nod.

"Do you really though?" she asks, her hands on her hips as she glares at me with what can only be described as mom-eyes.

This time, I shrug.

"Seraphine. We. Love. You." She guides me over to one of the waiting room chairs, away from the prying eyes of the nosy ladies of town, who are no doubt watching my train wreck with rapt interest.

"You're hurting, I get it. When Grams died, it felt like someone cleaved out a part of my soul. Like you and your daddy, she was literally all I had. I remember, so vividly, in the weeks after she passed, I wanted to follow after her, if only to bring her back and yell at her for leaving me. I spent weeks in this deep, dark pocket of grief. It felt like a personal affront to me that the world kept turning without her living.

"I was angry and mean and lashed out at anyone who tried to help. Thank God AzzyJo stuck with me, or I might've never come around."

"True story," Azalea cuts in. "Sister-girl was a damn mess, but look at her now. A business owner, a wife, a mama. It's okay to miss your daddy and to grieve, but don't let it swallow you whole."

"Yeah," I say hoarsely. "Okay."

"Are you sure you don't wanna come stay with Simon and me?" Magnolia asks, kneeling on the floor in front of me so we're eye level.

Just like the first time she asked, I want so badly to say yes, but some sick and twisted combination of pride and pigheadedness has me declining her offer.

"I promise you won't be putting us out. We have a guest room and everything."

"I know y'all do, Mags, but I need to learn to be on my own."

My cousin stares at me for a beat before rising back to her full height. "If you change your mind, the offer stands, 'kay?"

The bells over the door tinkle, saving me from having to reply.

"Oh, good, you're here," Myla Rose says, hopping up from the chair next to me to go to her husband.

"Glad to see you, too, darlin'," Cash says, wrapping his

muscled arms around her. He holds her to his chest with his face pressed into the space between her neck and shoulder. It's such a tender moment that it makes my heart ache a little more, knowing there's no one out there to hold me like that.

After he releases her, Cash turns to me. "I'm sorry for your loss, Seraphine. Dave'll be missed."

"Thanks," is all I can squeak out without breaking down again.

"Why don't we get you home?" Cash holds his hand out, presumably for my keys, which I pass him. He pockets them and extends his arm down again. I stare at it dumbly before Azalea clues me in.

"He's trying to help you up, girl."

"Oh." I feel my cheeks heat to nuclear levels.

I place my hand in his, and he hauls me to standing with ease. And, the gentleman that he is, Cash walks us out to Bertha, Myla's mint-green Land Cruiser. He opens the passenger door for me before walking his wife around to the driver's side.

He presses his lips to hers in a completely-indecent-for-public kiss, breaking it only when a random catcall from across the street rings out. "I love you, darlin'. I'll follow behind."

"Love you, too," she replies breathlessly as she joins me in the cab.

A wistful sigh escapes me as she cranks the engine. I hope the sound of the crankshaft turning and the pistons firing is enough to cover it, but luck's not on my side.

"What's the sigh for?"

"I don't know. Nothing... everything?" I shrug and rest my head against the cool glass of the window.

"Talk to me, Seraphine. It's not healthy to hold it all in."

"It's just… between the salon and taking care of Dad, I never really dated or anything. When Dad was healthy, the boys were all scared of him, and when he started getting ill, I just didn't have the time for it. And now, it's just… me."

God, could I sound any more pathetic?

"I'm gonna give you a little tough love, 'kay?"

"Sure."

"I was your age when I got pregnant with Brody. I was single and alone and scared shitless. I remember sobbing when I saw those two pink lines. And then I did what Grams would've told me to do—I put on my big girl panties, pulled myself up by my bootstraps, and dealt with it."

"I remember." I roll my head against the back of the seat to look at her. "But what does that have to do with me?"

"You need to pull yourself up, sister. I know your daddy's death is fresh and that you're hurting something fierce. I get it—I do. But I also know Dave wouldn't want to see you like this."

I turn back to the window, not wanting to hear her, even though she's right. If Dad was here, he wouldn't hesitate to tell me what an idiot I was being.

"Look, I know you don't wanna hear this. You're hurting and angry, and you have every right to be." She turns into my driveway and throws Bertha into park. "But you *need* to hear it all the same. It is okay to grieve, to mourn, to miss him. It is not okay to throw your life away. You said it yourself at his funeral, that your daddy always said *'it's what you do while you're alive that matters.'* Well, Seraphine, you're still alive—act like it."

In my heart of hearts, I know she is right and speaking from a place of love. Unfortunately, my brain and heart aren't on the same page. "Thanks for the ride."

She sighs. "You're welcome. Take the week off and we'll go from there."

"Sure thing." I unbuckle and throw open the door. "Bye."

Myla Rose gives me a long, sad look before backing out of the driveway so Cash can park my car. He drops my keys into my waiting hand before climbing into his wife's car.

They don't drive away until I'm safely inside, alone once again.

2

SERAPHINE

"Five." The pungent liquid splashes into my mouth, but I no longer taste it.

"Six." Another glug brings me that much closer to sweet oblivion.

"Seven." A bead of amber liquid drips down my chin with my final swallow—one for each day that's passed since they lowered my dad's body into the ground.

Once Dad's beer ran out, I started in on the liquor cabinet. Whatever's in this bottle—I didn't even bother to look—makes the beer seem like water. This is my first taste of straight-up alcohol; the first sip had me coughing and sputtering with tears in my eyes. But now, the bottle's nearly empty, my taste buds are numb, and I'm all cried out.

A painful mash-up of past memories and future wishes race through my foggy mind, out of control, swirling like angry white-water rapids.

I sink farther into the couch as wave after wave of *should-haves* crash over me. My dad *should have* lived long enough to see me married. He *should have* had a whole gaggle of grandbabies to call him Papa. He *should have* just… been here—too bad all of these *should-haves* were stolen from me with a mouthful of pills.

My eyelids droop as I give up fighting the current of my thoughts. I'm nearly down for the night when my phone starts vibrating in my back pocket with a notification. I'm half tempted to ignore it—but I don't.

Lord knows, if it's one of the girls from the salon, and I ignore them, they'll call in the calvary to deal with me. I've done my best to avoid the concerned trio—evading them with texts full of emojis that hopefully mask the self-destructive path I'm on.

Truly, I'm a mess. A sad, sloppy, angry mess.

Lucky for me, it's no one. Just a calendar notification. I move to swipe it away, but draw up short at the words on the screen.

No… surely not. I squint and move my phone closer to make sure I'm reading it right.

"Fuck, how could I…" I mumble to myself as I try to sit upright. Clumsily, I double-check the date. But my phone is right. The fair starts tonight, and for the past eighteen years, Dad and I have gone to the opening night.

It's our little tradition. We'd walk the block to the fairground, kick off the night with a corn dog, ride all of the rides, and end it with cotton candy.

Before I can think better of it, I'm up from the couch, shoving my feet into the first shoes I see, and stumbling out the door.

Looks like tonight, I'll be carrying out our tradition on my own.

The lights and sounds of the fair wrap around me, the familiarity a much-needed comfort. Even the smells— fried food, cow manure, and bad decisions—put me a little more at ease.

I wander around, taking it all in before finding the courage to kick off the first of what will surely be my new normal—*aloneness.*

On unsteady feet, with my newly acquired foot-long corn dog in hand, I make my way over to the small food tent. I claim a rickety plastic table and dig in, ready to make the best of things, except the golden-fried goodness tastes like ash in my mouth without Dad here to enjoy it with me.

Instead of arguing over which condiment is supreme, I'm eating in silence, wondering how in the hell it's possible for the world to keep spinning without Dad here.

My whole life, he's been this larger-than-life persona. That he's no longer here is unfathomable. The fact that he left of his own volition—it's nearly debilitating.

I'm dragging my corn dog through my ketchup and mustard mixture when a shadow falls over my table. "What's a pretty girl like you doing all alone?"

I glance up to find not one but two guys standing over my table. They're nearly interchangeable in looks—tall, fit, fishing shorts, button-downs, and university-affiliated ball caps. The only discernable difference is their hair color—one blond and one brunette.

"Eating?" My reply comes out as a question.

"Mind if me and my buddy here join you? All of the other tables are full."

A quick look around confirms the dark-haired man's statement. "Sure."

The two men sandwich me in. "Thanks. We got one more joining us."

"Okay," I say. In truth, I feel a little on edge with them here, but at the same time, it's so nice to be around people —people who don't know about the death of my dad. People who won't look at me with pity.

"A lady of few words, huh?" the blond asks.

I shrug.

"I'm Jason," the first man says.

"And I'm Allen."

"Seraphine," I say, my lips tipping up in a small grin.

"It's very nice to meet you," Jason says right as another man joins us. He's another carbon copy of his friends, except he's rocking a five-o'clock shadow and has his hat turned around backward.

"I brought beer!" the newcomer hollers before claiming the chair across from me.

"Manners," Allen chides, reaching for one of the plastic cups in the middle of the table.

"Well, hello there," he says in a voice that can only be described as a purr. "I'm lucky."

"That's your name?"

"No, Cliff's the name; I'm lucky because I get to spend my night with a beautiful woman such as yourself."

Despite the fall chill in the air, warmth blossoms across my cheeks.

"You want a drink?" Jason asks.

Warning bells—albeit very distant ones—sound, telling me not to take the drink. And yet, I find myself nodding and bringing the cup to my lips. My face screws up at the first sip, making them all laugh. There's nothing worse than cheap beer, and after seven days of drinking Dad's alcohol, the difference in quality has never been more apparent.

Still, these three and their booze may just prove to be the perfect distraction.

"One more!" Jason says, his cheeks ruddy from the nip in the air and the previous two rounds of drinks. I open my mouth to protest, but he's faster. "Just one more round and then we can check out the rides."

My initial protest dies on my lips when I see the pleading looks on my new friends' faces. "Okay, fine." A chorus of cheers ring out. "But only one!"

"You heard the lady," Allen whoops, sending Jason off to the drink tent.

The three of us talk—well, they talk, I listen—about a whole lot of nothing while we wait on Jason to return. About ten minutes later, he does, and we all throw our drinks back before tossing the cups and heading out toward the rides.

"Shiiiiit," I slur, swaying like a reed as we walk toward the Ferris wheel. "Those—" I stumble, and the pretty blond one catches me. "Thanks… y-yeah."

His lips are quirked up in a sinful smile. "I've got you." He hauls me back to standing but doesn't release me. "We've *all* got you."

I try to smile, but something about his words, even through the alco-haze, seems off. "St-strong."

He flexes a little. "I am."

"Strong d-drinks." My tongue feels fat—like it's too big for my mouth.

Blondie replies, but his voice is nothing more than a warble, as if he's on dry land and I'm underwater.

"Huh?" I murmur, wondering when my three new friends doubled to six.

The three—*or six*—men talk as they corral me to whatever destination they have in mind.

The sound of someone calling my name tickles my ears, but I'm too busy floating... too busy flying to reply.

Ser-a-phine. My name reaches me again, this time louder. I twirl in a circle, searching out the shouter of the syllables. The move sends both me and my blond man-friend flying to a heap on the ground.

He grumbles beneath me, but it's feminine hands that reach down to help me up.

Her mouth moves, but her words barely penetrate the haze around me—that is until she grabs me by the front of my shirt and forcibly pulls me to standing.

"Whoa!" I giggle at the sensation of falling upward. "Again!" I try and collapse back down, but someone supports me from behind. I try to turn to see who's at my back, but my newest friend isn't having it.

"Seraphine!" she yells, turning my face back to hers.

"Des-Desi?" I ask. "You g-got some splainin' to do!"

Her face pinches and mine falls. I think she's mad at me. "Are you m-mad at me?"

"Are you high?" she asks. Her voice sounds like a mom —or at least how I think a mom would sound—and not a high schooler. *Like a teen mom...* I crack up at my own joke. "Seriously, what's going on?"

"I'm good." My head rolls back, landing with a thump

on what has to be a man chest. A quick glance to the upper-right confirms it—my dark-haired friend is at my back. "Gooder than good. I'm grrrreat!"

She scoffs. "You sound blitzed, Tony the Tiger. Who are the dude-bros?"

I pinch my eyes closed as a wave of dizziness overtakes me. Jason starts rubbing his fingers over my exposed arms, and I shiver. "Uhhh. Friends?"

She mutters something under her breath and then Cliff steps in. "We were headed to the Ferris wheel, if you don't mind—"

"I do mind," Desi says, standing taller.

"Look, we don't want any trouble." Jason leans in and kisses my neck. "We just wanna take the lady for a ride."

The two other men snigger while I sag farther into his hold. My limbs feel like jelly and I think… no, I *know* if he keeps rubbing on me, I might just orgasm. My skin feels like there's a live-wire plugged into it and even the barest of touches is electric.

"I don't think—"

One of the guys cuts her off. "Listen, kid, this doesn't involve you."

A few more words are exchanged, but I'm too busy watching all of the bright, pretty lights to listen. "Ooh! The funhouse!" I try to bounce on my feet, but the ground moves under me. Luckily, Jason catches me.

"Seraphine—"

Now I'm the one cutting her off. "Have a fun time, Desi!"

The guys guide me away from Desi and toward the funhouse, murmuring to themselves all the while. It takes two of them to keep me upright. "Strong… drinks…" I murmur, nausea churning in my gut as they guide us into the line for the attraction. "So strong."

"She's good, man," one of them says.

"Mmm," the one at my back rumbles his agreement.

"G-good for what?" I ask, my teeth chattering, even though I'm sweating.

"Everything, baby girl, everything."

3

MATEO

I'VE GOT THE HOUSE TO MYSELF, A BOWL OF *FRIJOLES charros*—leftovers sent home from my mamá—an ice-cold beer, and a rerun of *Bitchin' Rides* playing on the flat screen.

Tonight's a rare night alone and the house is quiet. *Too quiet.* Without my motormouth here, flapping her gums. I joke that I'd pay her to be quiet, even for only five minutes, and yet with her being out with her friends, I find myself missing her incessant chatter.

The kid keeps our house lively and fills the void and without it, I feel… almost empty. Shockingly, at sixteen, she still enjoys spending time with her old man, but I know my days are numbered. Soon enough, the allure of boys and parties and things of that nature will all far surpass dear old dad.

With a few hours to myself, I was tempted to hit up a bar—to seek out some companionship for the evening—but chasing tail is a younger man's game, and it's not like I'm going to bring a woman back here. Not when Desi will be home in a few short hours. I would never let her see me disrespect her mother that way—God rest her soul.

I'm four episodes in when my phone rings, blasting out some stupid pop song Desi picked out. I swipe to answer, and my daughter's worried voice fills my ear. "Dad…"

"*¿Qué pasa?*" I ask. *What's up?*

When she doesn't answer right away, I'm instantly alert.

"*Pollito*, are you okay?"

"Yeah, but Seraphine—Mr. McAllister's whatever—is here, and she…"

My heart slows when Desi says she's okay but revs right back up at the mention of the dark-haired beauty. "What about her?"

"I don't know. She seems… off. Like she's high or something, and she's with these three guys and they seemed shady. Up to no good. Like, Dad, they literally had to support her, because she couldn't stand. I tried saying hi and checking on her, but she just sort of looked right through me, and when she did answer me, she sounded *loca*. I think… I think she needs help, Dad."

I scrub a hand over my face, proud of Desi's compassion—she gets it from her mama. Seraphine isn't my responsibility, but I know Dave would check on my daughter in a heartbeat if the roles were reversed—at least that's the motivation I'm going with.

"I'm on my way." I stand and shove my feet into my boots and grab my keys from the counter. "And, Dez, keep an eye on her, but do *not* engage."

"Okay."

The drive to the fairgrounds is a quick one, but I know too fucking well that things can go south in a matter of seconds.

Thankfully the opening-day-rush is over, and I don't have to wait in line to park or purchase a ticket. I call Desi back once I pass the gates. *"¿Dónde estás?"* I ask the second the call connects.

This urge I have to get to Seraphine is both foreign and familiar all at once. For most of the time I've known her, she's just been Dave's daughter.

Then about two years ago, when my GTO beat Dave's at Barbeque and Bumpers—a semi-local car show—she decided to give me an earful about how her dad's car was twenty times better than mine, claiming I won on a technicality.

It was then, while she chewed me up one side and down the other, that my fascination with the little spitfire started. But that's a secret I'll be taking to my grave. I'm *almost* old enough to be her father.

"I'm next to the spaceship. Dad, you gotta hurry. They're almost to the front of the line for the funhouse."

"On my way."

"Okay," she says on a shuddery exhale. "But, Dad, hurry." The worry in her voice ratchets up my own. Any other teen, and I'd assume they were worried over missing out on time with friends, but not my Desi. While she's got a wild hair about her, she's got a heart of gold, and I know her concern is genuine and warranted.

I shoulder my way through the crowd, wishing like hell it would part for me like the Red Sea did for Moses.

"Desi!" I cup my hands around my mouth to amplify my voice. My daughter's eyes fly to mine before darting to the left. I follow her line of sight, and sure enough, three people back from the entrance is Seraphine, surrounded by a trio of very recognizable dipshits.

As hard as it is, I manage to keep my composure as I approach, bypassing the line entirely. Dipshit *numero uno* —Jason—sees me first.

"Mateo, my man!" His hand shoots in the air, waving me over. "Como est-ass?" he shouts, butchering my native tongue like the disrespectful little fucker he is.

I nod, acknowledging him while assessing the situation. Seraphine can hardly stand up straight, her pupils are blown wide, and she's chewing on her inner-cheek something fierce. She's clearly rolling; meanwhile, dipshits one through three are all far more sober than she is.

"*Hijo de puta*," I growl before turning my attention back to the sad excuse of a man standing before me. "Who's your friend?" I figure I'll play dumb—for now.

"This little bow-nita is our friend for the night." He wags his brows. "If you catch my drift."

I ball my hands into tight fists and grit my teeth. "Does she have a name?"

Jason rolls his eyes. "Yeah, man. It's… uh…"

Dipshit doesn't even know her name.

"It's Serenade," the one I haven't met yet says smugly.

"No, it's not," dipshit two—Cliff—argues.

"Is, too."

"Nah, man, it totally is, right, baby?"

As if coming out of a trance, Seraphine blinks and turns to face the *idiota*. "Sure, I'm whoever you want me to be."

25

Her words sound like they're ants trudging through molasses, slow and heavy.

"Seraphine!" I bite out her name, my tone sharper than I intended for it to be.

Her eyes widen at the sight of me. "Mmmm-Mateo," she practically moans my name.

"I knew you had it wrong!" Cliff shouts, pulling Seraphine out of his friend's arms and into his. It takes my all not to throttle him when I see his thumb dip below the waistband of her jeans.

"You know her?" Jason asks, stepping slightly in front of her, like he has some sort of claim to her.

"I do." I take a step closer. "She's a friend"—I arrange my lips into a smirk, even though I'm not really feeling it—"a *really good* friend." I should feel bad for playing up our relationship, but I don't. Not even a little, because God only knows what these *bastardos* have planned.

"Oh, yeah?"

As fast as lightning, I reach out and steal her away from Cliff. She throws her arms around my neck and squeals at the sudden motion. "Whoa!" She looks up at me and tries batting her lashes—though, it looks more like she's trying to tap out a message in Morse code with her eyes.

"You good, *mariposita*?"

A little sigh slips past her lips as she leans into me, locking her arms around my middle. "You smell so good." She presses her face into my chest and breathes in deeply. "Like after a storm and sweaty sex."

"*Ay Dios mio,*" I mutter under my breath, trying to stop her roaming hands.

Dipshit number three chuckles. "Looks like our good time just became yours, man."

Jason elbows his friend, but he keeps talking.

"You gonna baby her like you do our trucks? Or maybe be a little more rou—"

I snap. Well, more accurately, his head snaps back after my fist connects with his jaw. "*Tu verga caida pedazo de mierda!*" I roar, winding my arm back to hit him again.

"What the fuck?" Cliff shouts, stepping up to me with his chest bowed out, like I won't knock his ass out, too.

I continue going off, switching between Spanish and English as my emotions get the better of me.

"Jesus Christ, man!" Jason yells, putting himself between me and his friends, knowing good and well I won't lay a hand on him. "Chill the fuck out and speak fucking English. You're in America."

I twist my head down and to the side until my neck cracks. "You want to know what I was saying?"

Seraphine wiggles in my arms, giggling to herself. "So hot, always speak Spanish."

Ignoring her, I plow straight ahead. "I said you and your friends are pathetic, limp-dicked pieces of shit. You gotta drug a girl to get some action? Pathetic."

"Now hold on," Jason says, sounding just like his smooth-talking judge father. "Where on earth did you get the notion that we drugged her? Seems more likely she overindulged, doesn't it? And take a look at her outfit. Dressed like that, she's asking for trouble." He clicks his tongue at me. "If anything, you should *thank us* for taking such good care of your girl. God only knows what trouble might have befallen her without us."

While unspoken, the threat in his words is clear. If I

lay a finger on him, he'll call his dad. If I report him and his friends to the authorities, it'll be my word against his —and the word of tatted-up, brown-skinned mechanic against that of a college-educated, richer than God white boy with a judge for a dad… yeah, the math isn't too hard.

"Thanks, then." I grind out the words, wishing like hell I could knock his punk-ass out without a hefty fine and probable jail sentence. "We'll be on our way."

I steer Seraphine away from the crowd of onlookers, catching Desi's eye as we pass her. She nods before she and her group of friends continue on their way.

By the time we make it to the parking lot, Seraphine's practically rubbing her body against mine like a cat in heat, mumbling God knows what under her breath.

"Did you drive here?" I ask, my voice harsher than I intended.

She releases me from her hold and spins to face me. Her eyes are the size of saucers, and her lips are working a mile a minute. Her lips part as if to answer me, but instead a soft sigh escapes her lips and she reaches a hand up to rub at the scruff on my face.

Gently, I knock her hand away and make a mental note to get her something to chew on so she doesn't eat her cheeks raw.

"Seraphine, did you drive here?"

She shakes her head back and forth lazily before falling face-first into my chest.

"Let's get you inside," I murmur, moving her back to an upright position.

"No, let's get *you* inside… me." Her voice is a lazy drawl that sends shivers up my spine—and not the good kind. To hear her talk like this is unnerving, and the thought of how this night could've have ended without Desi's intervention is downright terrifying.

"Inside the car, *mariposita*, the car."

I unlock my truck with my free hand and swing open the passenger side door. She squeals as I pluck her off the ground and swing her up into the cab. "Ooh, dizzy." She flings herself against the seatback.

"You good?" Despite the flush in her cheeks, she's looking a little green around the gills.

"Mmm-nun-uh," she mumbles before buckling over and puking all over my floorboard.

I do my best to smooth her hair away from her face, whispering words of comfort to her, all the while trying not to think about what it'll take to get the stench of her vomit out of my ride.

After one final heave, Seraphine rights herself, wiping the back of her hand over her mouth as she sits up. "Oh, wow." She smacks her lips. "That was gross—oh! Mateo, shit. Sorry. About your truck. And stuff."

She's talking a mile a minute now.

"Feel better?"

"Soooo much. Like really good. Great."

It's going to be a long fucking night is all I can think as I lean into the cab to pull her seat belt across her, trying like hell not to gag. "Good. Let's get outta here."

"Where are we going?" she asks, bouncing in the seat like a small child.

"*Loca*," I mutter, shaking my head as I close her door and round the front of the truck to the driver's side.

4

SERAPHINE

"Wake up, *mariposita*," a deep voice whispers in my ear, pulling me away from the most fucked-up dream I've had in a while—it involved the fair, frat boys, and Mateo—*oh, shit.*

I try to ask why he's in my bed, but nothing more than a croak comes out as pain robs me of my ability to speak.

"Take your time," he says from his spot beside me.

I roll my lips inward as I let saliva pool in my mouth. The pain is reminiscent of adjusting to braces, only worse. Thankfully, after a few beats, I'm able to get my voice to work, even if it does come out raspy and raw. "Why are you in my bed?"

"I'm not," he says, grinning. "You're in mine."

It's then I notice the unfamiliar surroundings. Instead of being in my double bed, cocooned in my fluffy white duvet, I'm sprawled out in the middle of a plush, king-sized bed, tucked under the softest gray blanket to ever exist.

"Oh, God. It wasn't a dream?" It's a stupid question,

because there's certainly no other reason for me to find myself waking up anywhere near Mateo, much less *in* his bed.

A quick peek beneath the covers confirms my fears— I'm clad in a pair of should-never-see-the-light-of-day yoga shorts and a threadbare T-shirt, sans bra. Which means, not only has Mateo seen me in this getup, but so has most of the damn town.

"What wasn't?"

I groan and pull one of the spare pillows over my heated cheeks to hide my shame. "Everything. All of it."

He pulls my fluffy shield away and gently turns my face toward him. "How do you feel? I've got water and Tylenol for you on the nightstand and coffee in the kitchen."

"Like I got hit by a bus…" I try to recall the details of last night, but I can only grasp bits and pieces. "Or made a lot of bad decisions."

"Eh." He shrugs. "Maybe a little bit of both, you know, if you consider going out and getting drugged being hit by a bus."

"Drugged?" I sit up so fast our foreheads knock together. "Ouch."

"*Mujer cabeza dura.*" Mateo rubs at the spot where our skulls collided.

"What?"

"Nothing." He passes me the bottle of water along with the Tylenol bottle. "Are you okay?"

After hearing I was drugged, the fact that both items are still sealed doesn't escape my notice. If anything, it makes my heart pitter-patter in my chest a little harder, which is stupid because it's not like a *man* like him would ever take notice of me.

Mateo Reyes is a tatted-up, golden-skinned Spanish-speaking devil of a man whose voice alone sends shivers down my spine. I've been enamored with him since I was a kid, but he's never paid much attention to me—except the one time I went psycho on him after he beat my dad in a race. I regretted it instantly, but earlier that morning we found my dad's health had taken *another* turn for the worse.

Basically, I needed an outlet for my pain, and he was there.

"Yes… I think so." I stop and take stock of my body. Aside from the mouth pain and a minor headache, I don't feel any worse for wear. "Why does the inside of my mouth feel like raw meat?"

"*Tachas,*" Mateo sighs.

"Huh?"

"Ecstasy, mariposa, I'm pretty sure they slipped you ecstasy."

A kaleidoscope of scenarios flash through my mind, each one more horrifying than the last. Those guys could have done anything to me—they could have freaking gang-raped me, and I would have been helpless to stop it.

"Hey, shh, you're okay." Mateo wraps his strong arms around me and draws me close. "I've got you, you're safe."

I don't even realize I'm crying until my tears have soaked through his shirt.

"Sorry," I offer with a forced grin, swiping at my cheeks.

"Do not apologize." He nods down to the bottles in my lap. "Take two."

"Thanks." My hands tremble, but I do as he says, passing both bottles back to him once I'm finished.

"What do you remember?"

"I was home and sad and drinking. And I was about to go to bed when I realized it was the first night of the fair, so I… yeah." I expect him to tell me I'm an idiot, for him to lecture me like my own father would have at any moment, but Mateo simply nods for me to continue. "I got a corn dog, and then those guys approached me. I was leery, but they seemed all right. They took turns doing beer runs. It gets a little fuzzy after that."

"Are you even old enough to drink?" He squints at me, as if he's mentally doing the math.

I look down at my hands, ashamed. "No," I whisper.

He reaches over with a tender touch, once again turning my face back to his. "Don't."

"Don't what?" I ask, my voice barely audible over the sound of my heartbeat whooshing in my ears.

"Don't blame yourself and don't think I am judging you." His eyes lock on to mine in a way that feels like he's peering into my soul. I squirm under the weight of his dark stare, but Mateo doesn't relent. "The only people to blame are those low-life assholes who drugged you. I don't care if you were drinking and wearing revealing clothing. Hell, you could have been butt-ass naked and it still wouldn't have given them the right. You did not consent to taking drugs, Seraphine, and that's that."

"That's that?" I echo back, doubt still eating away at me. The thought of someone—multiple someones—potentially violating me has my skin crawling and my gut churning.

"*Sí.*" He says the word with such conviction that I don't

question him any further, even if I'm not so sure I agree. I mean, it's hard not to let doubt creep in. Day in and day out, girls and women hear about how they shouldn't have put themselves in the situation or dressed in such a way. Nine times out of ten, the blame falls on the woman, and I can't help but wonder, if Mateo hadn't come along, what would my odds have been?

Beneath all of my hurt and fear, I know Mateo's right. Yes, I acted irresponsibly, and I fully own that. However, that still doesn't give anyone the right to drug me. Plain and simple.

"Hey, Mateo?" I nibble my lip, torn on whether or not I should ask the question burning the back of my throat.

"Yeah?"

"How did I end up here?"

He mutters in Spanish under his breath before answering me. "Desi saw you, talked to you, and was worried. She called me."

"You… you came there just for me?" I know I sound like a silly girl with stars in her eyes, but I don't care. The knowledge that Mateo knew I was in trouble and came for me only serves to fan the flame of the silly crush I've always harbored for him.

"Dave would've done the same for Desi."

His words instantly reduce my inferno down to embers, and while it hurts, it's the reminder I need. I am nothing to this man other than an old friend's daughter. He'll never see me as more, and it would serve me well to remember that.

"Right, yeah," I whisper, trying not to sound as dejected as I feel. Instead of wallowing, I square my shoulders and carry on like my cheeks aren't burning with shame. "So, anything else I need to know about? Did I do anything totally humiliating?"

Mateo's eyes flash, and I know I did something, but he simply shakes his head.

"Are you sure?"

"Don't worry about it. Let's just get you fed, and home." He stands and crosses the room to his dresser. "Throw these on and come to the kitchen—down the hall and to the left."

I nod, not trusting myself to speak. In addition to being seen as a child, I'm an inconvenience he can't wait to rid himself of. Maybe I should skip breakfast, sneak out, and hoof it home?

I'm one leg into the gray sweats he tossed at me when I realize I have no idea where he lives. Knowing my luck, his house is probably clear across town from mine.

Resigned, I finish pulling them on. I'm fairly tall, but the pants still hang off of my hips. I roll them a few times, finger comb my hair into a semi-presentable state, swish with his mouthwash, and set off in search of the kitchen and the coffee he promised me.

I take my time moving through the house, taking note of the pictures lining the walls. Desi is everywhere—her entire life from birth to now is displayed in this hallway. There are also pictures of what I assume is Mateo's family, as well as a few of a stunning black woman who is the spitting image of Desi. "Must be her mother," I murmur to myself.

"It is," says a feminine voice behind me, causing me to jump.

Whirling around, I find myself face-to-face with Mateo's daughter. My cheeks heat as she looks me over.

I'm not sure if I'm more embarrassed for her to see me in her dad's clothes or to catch me openly snooping.

At a loss for words, I nod.

"Her name's Imani. She died when I was little —cancer."

Tears sting my eyes. "I'm sorry," I whisper, not knowing what else to say. Hell, there really isn't anything else. I know good and well words can't bring back those we loved... nothing can.

Desi shrugs. "Don't be. I mean, yeah, it sucks and all, but I know she loved me."

"Right. Yeah." This girl has me at a total loss for words. "That's... um..."

She shakes her head at me, a small smile playing on her lips. "C'mon. If we're lucky, Dad will make *huevos revueltos a la Mexicana.*"

"Eggs?" I ask lamely.

Desi nods. "Yeah, but better."

She takes off down the hall, but I hesitate. "Hey," I call after her.

"Yeah?"

"Thanks." I shrug, unsure of how to properly thank someone for doing what she did. "For... you know."

"No worries; us girls gotta stick together, right?"

"Right." Desi nods, her lips tipped up in a knowing grin. "Good. Now, let's eat."

She turns and heads down the hall—presumably toward the kitchen. I take my time following after her, needing a few minutes to get my wits about me before facing Mateo.

I pause just before the threshold at the sound of Mateo's voice. "What's got you grinning?" I hear him ask.

After a pause, Desi replies, "Things and stuff."

"Things and stuff, huh?"

"Yup. Stuff and things." Listening to the two of them volley back and forth reminds me so much of Dad and me. Up until he couldn't, he was always so invested in all things me. Even when he was in hospice, he'd use what little energy he had to ask me about my day, about boys, about life in general.

"Swear to God, you're just like your mama." The fondness in Mateo's voice makes my heart ache in the most bittersweet of ways. Here I am, crushing over a man who's already had his great love.

"Thanks, Dad."

I decide to make my entrance, not wanting to take advantage of their hospitality by eavesdropping—well, any more than I already have.

Mateo hones in on me the second I enter the room. He parts his lips, as if to speak, but no words come out. He looks me up and down with a stare so heavy it feels like a physical caress.

My skin turns to gooseflesh under his scrutiny, and I can't help but let my imagination run wild with what he might be thinking.

Is he imagining shoving the dishes from the table and tossing me down on it, or is he merely wondering when he'll get these pants back from me?

Who can say—but with the way he's biting on his bottom lip, I'm willing to bet it's closer to the *feasting on me* option.

He's practically in a trance until Desi claps her hands together mere centimeters from his face.

"*Dios mio,* Desi!" Mateo yells, but there's no heat behind his words.

The teen girl doesn't look even the least bit sorry. If anything, she looks proud. "If you're done staring, I'd like some breakfast. *Huevos revueltos a la Mexicana, por favor.*"

My cheeks burn at her blunt observation—the fact that her dad might have just eye-fucked me in front of her is beyond mortifying.

I expect Mateo to correct her; instead, he gives me one last burning look before addressing his daughter. "Grab the eggs."

"Is there anything I can do to help?" I ask, feeling out of place.

Mateo shakes his head no, but Desi asks, "You know how to chop veggies?"

I nod.

"Great." Desi grabs two cutting boards from the drawer and two knives from the block. "You dice the onion and pepper and I'll do the tomato and cilantro."

"She's a guest," Mateo admonishes. "Seraphine, go and pour some coffee and rest."

"Um…" I'm like a deer caught in headlights. "I don't mind helping. Really, it's the least I could do."

Desi shoots her father a victorious grin and then, like we've been doing it forever, the three of us get to work chopping and dicing and scrambling until there's a skillet of sizzling eggs waiting to be devoured.

5

MATEO

Breakfast is a lesson in self-control. Hell, the entire morning has been—last night, too.

From the moment I knew she was safe, I wanted to look—to drink my fill of her in those damn booty shorts. Especially when she was sprawled out on my bed, begging for my touch in her drugged state.

However, my mamá didn't raise no *cabrón*, and I'd never take advantage of a woman in her state. But when she walked into the kitchen in my sweats, all bets were off. I realized Seraphine Reynolds is a thirst I'll never quench.

I don't know if it's because she's the first woman I've seen in my clothes since Imani, but the sight of it short-circuited my brain and had all of my baser caveman instincts clawing their way to the surface.

I wanted to do more than look; I wanted to touch—to feel her soft, tanned skin beneath my calloused hands. The way the rolled waistband sat low on her slim hips, all

I could think about was how easy it'd be to slide them down her toned legs.

More than that though, I wanted to taste—to part her pretty little thighs and bury my face between them and feast. Until Desi clapped in front of my face, I was a simpleton with a single focus in mind—*claim her.*

Which is problematic for a slew of reasons.

"Oh, God, I didn't know eggs could be so good," Seraphine mumbles quietly to herself, prompting me to go over said reasons again, for what has to be the tenth time this morning.

A man shouldn't think these types of thoughts about the daughter of a man they call a friend—even if it is in a more professional capacity.

A man especially does not think these thoughts in front of his own daughter.

These are definitely not the thoughts a man has for a woman sixteen years younger than him, one not even old enough to legally drink.

And yet, here I am, having every single one of them—and then some. It's all too easy to imagine her here with us every morning. While Seraphine has certainly caught my attention, she's never evoked such a visceral response.

"Aren't they the best?" Desi agrees, all sunshine and smiles, which is curious because the kid is usually a beast in the mornings.

The dark-haired beauty may as well be a mirage in the desert or a poisoned well, because one sip, one drop, one taste, and I know I'll be a goner.

Seraphine takes one last bite before pushing her plate away. "I could literally eat them every day. Wow."

"If you think these are good, you should have my *abuelita's chilaquiles.* No lie, they'll change your life."

She regards Desi thoughtfully. "I'm not sure what that is, but I can't imagine anything better than this."

Desi goes to reply, but I beat her to the punch. "You're good for a man's ego, *mariposita*, but let's get you home."

My daughter's eyes widen, and I realize my slip. *Mariposita.* I'm not sure when I started calling her that, but damn, to do it here, in front of Desi…

"Oh, um, yeah. Do… should I help clean up?"

"Nah, we got it," I assure her.

"I'm gonna—I need to use the restroom before we leave."

Desi nods her head back toward the hall. "Second door on the left."

Seraphine nods her thanks and takes off down the hall.

"Little butterfly, huh?" Desi asks with barely disguised glee.

"I don't know, Des. It just… slipped out."

"I'm just saying, you call her little butterfly and me little chicken."

I grin. "I cannot help you there; your *abuelita* gave you that name. Take it up with her."

"Do you like her?"

"Who?" I play dumb. "My own mother? Yes, I love her."

"No, Dad, *Seraphine*. Do you like her?"

Silence rules as I grapple with how to respond. Ultimately, I go for honesty. "I don't know. I'm… attracted to her." *Dios mio,* this is not something I want to talk about with my daughter. "But I do not plan to act on that attraction. You have nothing to worry about."

Desi rolls her eyes and mutters under her breath, "Except you dying old and alone."

"What was that?"

"You're still young, Dad, and Mom would want you to be happy."

Her words rankle. "I am happy, *pollito.* I have you."

"I love you, Dad, but you need more than me. You need someone just for you. In two years, I'll be off to college and then what?" She crosses her arms and stares me down. "Plus, it might be kind of nice to have a woman in the house, right?"

I scrub a hand over my face. I never knew she felt like this. Have I failed her somehow by not providing a motherly figure? "Des—" I start, but she cuts me off.

"I'm not saying you have to go out and marry her and put a bun in her oven; I'm just saying I'm not opposed to you dating."

"She's too young," I say dismissively, right as she walks back into the room.

"Um, I'm ready." Seraphine looks down at her feet. "To go… home."

I don't know if she heard me or not, but judging from the wounded-puppy look she's got going on, I'm guessing she did. I won't feel guilty, though, because it's true. Regardless of how tempting she is—*very*—she's too young. Too naïve. Too immature. She's impulsive and reckless and probably not the best role model for Desi.

"Great, let me grab my keys."

I run back to my bedroom and grab the keys to my

GTO, since my truck still needs a thorough cleaning. As I head back to the kitchen, my phone dings with a text.

Desi: Age is just a number.

Swear to God, this kid… she's going to have me gray long before college.

By the time I get back to the kitchen, Desi is nowhere in sight, and Seraphine is standing by the island waiting for me.

"You ready?"

"Yup," she replies, not meeting my gaze.

"Everything okay?"

"Never been better." The bite in her tone catches me off guard; it's a stark contrast to the curl of her shoulders and the way she's looking at everything except me.

I cock my head to the side as I study her, waiting to see a glimpse of the fiery woman I've come to know.

Instead, she gives me her back, tossing a *let's go* gesture over her shoulder.

Knowing it's in my best interest not to push her, I follow along—until she realizes she doesn't know where she's going. "The hall on the left," I tell her, still letting her lead.

She pauses at the door to the garage, and I crowd her from behind, reaching around her to open the door. For a fleeting instant, I'm struck with the vision of spinning her to face me, hoisting her against the door, and devouring those pouting lips of hers like a man possessed.

I settle for resting my hand at the small of her back as I guide her to my most prized possession—the GTO that beat her dad's.

Seraphine scoffs when I hit the unlock button on the

fob. "A purist like your dad?" I ask, fighting the grin begging to break free.

"Some things are better left original."

"Whatever you say, *mariposita*." I open the door for her.

"Don't patronize me," she snaps as she lowers herself into the leather-wrapped bucket seat.

I hold up my hands in innocence. "I'm not." She glares, and I rush to add, "Truly, I'm not. We're all entitled to our own opinions. Your dad liked to keep things OG, and I prefer to modernize. There is no one right way."

"So now you're saying I don't have my own opinion?" She crosses her arms beneath her breasts, pushing them up in the most tempting of ways.

"What? No, I—"

She bursts out laughing. "Chill. I'm messing with you."

"*Malvada*," I mutter under my breath as I stalk around to the driver's side.

I turn the key and the engine roars to life. The sound alone—the deep, fierce growl—gives me chills every time. This car was originally a resto-mod for a buyer, but he backed out, and I decided to keep her for myself. It cost a small fortune to fix her up, but I have zero regrets.

"Buckle up." I check my mirrors and throw it into reverse.

"Yes, *sir*." Her emphasis on sir tells me she was being a sarcastic little shit, trying to make me feel old. The joke's on her though, because now, I'm imagining all of the other scenarios in which she could call me sir—and trust me, there are many.

"You still live over on Tupelo?"

"All my life."

I back out into the street, and Seraphine snorts out a laugh.

"What?"

"It's just"—she shakes her head—"you really do live clear across town. Go figure."

She's a little odd, this one. "Yeah, I guess I do. Wanted to be close to family." I don't know why I'm telling her this, but my gums keep flapping. "Especially when Imani got sick. It just seemed… easier, you know? To have help close by. *Mi mamá* and my sister, Silvia, live a block away, and Arrón is the house behind mine."

"Oh, yeah. Okay." She sounds about as confused as I am over the unwarranted info-dump.

"Tell me," I say, changing the subject, "what's going on with your dad's shop?"

In my periphery, I notice she balls her hands into tight fists in her lap. "What do you mean?"

"I mean, surely he had appointments and customers when he passed. What is going to happen to his shop?"

"Why do you care?" There's that petulance again, shining through to remind me of her age.

"I care because he was a good man who had damn near perfected his craft, and I know his customers are curious as well."

She huffs. "I don't know, okay? His lawyers and even a few customers keep calling the house, but I don't know what to tell them."

"Ignoring a problem won't make it go away, Seraphine."

"You think I don't know that?"

I flip on the blinker to turn onto her street. "I think

you're under a lot of stress and dealing with what feels like insurmountable grief. It's okay to need a little help."

"I don't need help."

"You do."

I pull into her driveway, taking note of how rundown the place looks. The once-pristine ranch-style home now shows its age. The yard is overgrown—practically a jungle —and the exterior is in need of a good pressure washing, probably even some paint. Judging from the state of the house, Dave was too unwell to care for it for a while.

I gesture to the scene before us. "Clearly you do."

Seraphine sniffs, and she unbuckles. "I've been busy."

She reaches for the door handle but I stop her. "Busy with what?"

"I don't really see how it's any of your business."

Disappointment has me shaking my head—though I'm not sure who I'm more disappointed in: me for basically shaming her for how she's dealing with the loss of her father or her for burying her head in the sand.

"You're right. I'm sorry." She gets out of the car, but I holler after her before she has a chance to swing the car door shut. "Just know—it doesn't make you weak."

"What doesn't?"

"Asking for help."

6

MATEO

I<small>T'S BEEN TWO WEEKS SINCE MY FAIRGROUND RESCUE,</small> and as loathe as I am to admit it, I haven't stopped thinking about Seraphine since. Damn bewitching woman has me under her spell.

So much so that I'm not even a little bit ashamed of my plans to fish for info from Simon when he stops by the shop this afternoon.

Until then, there's a lift kit with my name on it.

Countless hours later, my stomach rumbles, and I break to find food.

"Brother!" Arrón hollers from halfway across the garage as I head to the sink to scrub my hands. "You about done?"

"Not quite."

"It's been six hours."

I glance up toward the giant clock on the wall in disbelief. I worked straight through lunch, and Simon will be here shortly.

"*Chinga tu madre!*" I rack my brain trying to catalog the

contents of the fridge in the office. I didn't bring a lunch and don't have time to go anywhere.

"*¿Qué pasa?* What's wrong, brother?"

My stomach grumbles, answering Arrón for me.

"You're in luck." He grins.

I quirk a brow, gesturing for him to explain.

"I ran by *Jefecita's* and she made *enchiladas de mole.*"

"And you saved me some?" I'm already salivating, just imagining the taste. Nobody—and I mean that—is a better cook than my mother.

He pinches his thumb and forefinger together. "*Un poquito.*"

I crack a smile. "Better than none."

"I'm a real fucking saint." Arrón smirks, miming a halo over his head.

"Yeah." I turn and walk past him. "Saint Dipshit."

"Talk all the shit you want, Mate, but I could have eaten it all."

"Too true," I concede, holding the door to the office open for him.

The second I step foot into the room, the familiar scents of Mamá's kitchen greets me, causing my mouth to water.

"Is there rice?"

"Does a cow have spots?"

"Hell yes."

At the small corner table, I tear into the container Arrón brought, readily forking a mouthful of spicy-sweet goodness into my mouth. I groan in delight as I clean my plate. "Fuck, that is good."

"You kiss your mama with that mouth, Mateo?"

I turn toward the new voice, smiling ear to ear. "Simon —funny man."

"I'd like to think so," he says, pulling up a chair to the table.

"And I'd like to see you talk like that in front of *Jefa*." My brother laughs to himself. "She'd tear you up."

"Nah, she loves me too much."

"Whatever, everyone knows as the oldest, I'm her favorite; you're just the middle child."

"You lie and you know it," Arrón says with a chuckle, running a hand over his head.

"Yeah, Silvi is her favorite for sure," Simon adds. He's only been around them a handful of times, and even he knows our little sister wears the proverbial crown.

"Truth. The baby and the only girl." I pop the last bite of food in my mouth and turn to Simon, focusing my attention on him. "What's good with you?"

"Everything, man, but I gotta odd request for you."

"How odd?"

"I want to give Willow a custom Power Wheel for her birthday, and you're the man for the job."

Arrón and I both break into matching grins. "How custom?" he asks.

"Lift it a little, a brush guard bumper with a play wench, paint, decals, basically the works."

My brother and I are both howling with laughter now. "*Eres un loco hijo de puta.*"

"Crazy?" Simon asks. "Definitely. As for being the son of a bitch—jury's still out."

I freeze, worrying we've offended him, until he cracks up as well.

"So, can you do it?" he asks through his laughter.

Arrón mutters his questions back to him under his breath while I answer aloud. "We can do it. When do you need it?"

After we hammer out the details—from design to deadline—Simon asks, "Y'all think she'll like it? Right?"

Arrón claps him on the back. "Man, any kid would."

"I can't believe she's going to be three." His voice is wistful—the kind of voice a father reserves solely for his daughter.

"Desi will be seventeen her next birthday. My *pollito* is almost grown."

"If it's any consolation, she's a good kid. You've raised her right." Simon's eyes brighten. "Just the other day, there was a new kid—a transfer—and she was lost. Desi not only walked her to her class but drew her a map and highlighted the best routes. Like, she's just... a good kid."

My eyes burn, but I force a smile. "It's all Imani. She's her mama through and through."

"Don't sell yourself short, brother. You do your part."

We shoot the shit for a little more until Simon's phone trills in his pocket.

"Hey, Goldilocks, everything okay?" A pause. "Again? Have you tried calling... yeah, no, I know. You want me to ride out and check on her? You sure? Okay. Love you."

He sighs as he tosses his phone down onto the table.

"Everything okay?"

"Yeah, man, it's just... Seraphine has Mags crazy worried."

I clear my throat and prop my elbows on the tabletop, going for nonchalant. "Worried how?"

"She hasn't been to work since her dad passed. She's acting out—lashing out. Magnolia and the girls are obviously concerned. Hell, I'm concerned. Something's gotta give, but the girl is as stubborn as a mule."

"Did you hear about the fair?" Arrón asks, unknowingly baiting my hook for me.

Simon's brow furrows. "No…"

I give him the bare bones, not wanting to tell her business behind her back. However, the little I divulge is enough to have Simon smoking mad. "What the fuck?" he growls, shoving his chair back from the table so hard it nearly topples when he stands.

"She's okay. Desi actually called me, and I got there before anything happened."

"Mateo, man, I don't know what to say—how to repay you."

I wave my hands in front of my chest. "No repayment necessary."

He paces a few laps around the office, muttering to himself before turning to me. "You might change your mind after what I'm about to ask of you."

A strange combination of interest and dread mingle within me. "Which is?"

"Could you maybe like… check on her?"

The dread turns to some other emotion—one I'm not too keen to name. My friend here doesn't know it, but he's basically just given me the keys to the kingdom. Regardless of the fact that nothing will ever *be* between the two of us, a few heated looks and banter never hurt anybody.

"Check on her how?" I ask, making sure to keep a neutral tone.

Simon scratches his chin. "I don't know, it's just… she won't let Mags in. She barely even answers her calls, and you've sort of already *been there* for her. Maybe she'll be more receptive to you?"

My lips twitch with a smile, but I school my features before it can surface. "If you think it'll help."

Arrón sits silently, his phone in hand. To anyone else, he looks wholly engrossed in his screen. But I know him; I know he's listening to every word Simon and I exchange. Just like I also know, the second we're alone, he's going to give me shit—like he's been doing the past two years—for being attracted to her in the first place.

"I honestly don't know, but it can't hurt to try, right?"

Simon looks so hopeful, as if my intervention could somehow change everything for Seraphine. I'm not exactly sure that's true, but I also know I'm going to try my damndest to get through to her. I'm going to rally around her fine ass until she rejoins the land of the living, even if I have to drag her out of limbo myself.

The path she's on now leads to nothing but destruction, and if Simon thinks I can help, maybe I can. Our chemistry and harmless flirting aside, at this point, I don't think my conscience will let me not try, at the very least, to get through to her.

I sure as hell would want someone to step in and help Desi—though, preferably without thinking about her sexually.

I shake off the bout of nausea that rolls through me at the thought of anyone thinking of my daughter the way I think of Seraphine, take a cleansing breath, and turn to Simon. "I'll give it my best."

7

SERAPHINE

I FIGHT THE URGE TO CRY AS YET ANOTHER DEBT COLLECTOR calls. Apparently, Dad fell behind on the mortgage for the shop and put the house—*our home*—up as collateral. I know toward the end, he wasn't thinking clearly, but still, I find myself angry.

So very angry.

He could have at least told me, because now, it's on my shoulders, and a heads-up would've been great.

But since luck's rarely on my side, he never thought to mention how dire the finances were before ending his life.

I need money—and fast—if I want to keep a roof over my head, not to mention Dad's shop. Which means I need to start looking for a new job, seeing as I'm too chicken shit to show my face back at the salon after ghosting them for the last three weeks.

The worst part is, I know they'd welcome me back with open arms, and I still can't bring myself to do it.

Magnolia, Myla Rose, and Azalea have all left me countless voice mails and texts, all of which I've ignored.

The thought of talking to them—people who know and love me—makes it hard to breathe. Every time my phone dings, it's like my blood turns to sludge in my veins.

I'm pretty sure Simon's been by a time or two—or at least I assume it's him knocking on my front door—I wouldn't know since I hide in my bedroom whenever anyone knocks.

Hiding from all of my problems is proving a poor coping tactic, but I feel stuck.

So damn stuck.

It's like I'm in quicksand, and the more I try to figure everything out, the deeper into the pit I seem to sink.

"You can do this." I pace the length of the living room, trying to pump myself up to call Dad's lawyer. He's been trying to reach me since the day after Dad died, but like everyone else, the thought of talking to him makes me feel like I can't breathe. "Just pick up the phone and—"

I freeze at the sound of someone rapping on the front door, hoping they'll give up after a few seconds. But this time, the pounding keeps on.

"Seraphine, open the door!"

I know that voice... but why would he be here? Especially after three weeks of radio silence.

I creep over to the window and peek through the blinds. Sure enough, smack dab in the middle of my porch is Mateo Reyes, in all of his brooding glory. He's standing with his arms crossed and a frown on his face, looking as handsome as ever.

"I know you're here. Your car is in the driveway."

Still, I don't acknowledge his presence.

"The lights are on. Open the door, *mariposita*, or I'll open it for you."

I balk at his empty threat, half tempted to do as he says, if only to yell at him.

"You asked for it." I hear him mutter before the sound of the lock disengaging meets my ears.

"Oh my God!" I shriek as he flings the door open and steps into my home completely uninvited. "What are you doing? Get out!"

He pauses just over the threshold and takes me in, his dark eyes eating me up in a way that has shivers rolling down my spine.

"Put some clothes on."

I'm wearing the same shorts from the fair but with a bralette instead of a shirt. It's a perfectly acceptable ensemble to wear in the privacy of my own home, and really, it shows no more skin than a swimsuit would. Still, I fight the urge to cover myself. If this brute of a man thinks he can bust into my house uninvited and then boss me around, he's wrong.

"Don't like it?" I wave my hand up and down my body, showcasing the expanse of skin on display. "Then. Don't. Look."

Mateo growls low in his throat, like a wolf about to clamp its teeth around the throat of its prey. "Not liking it isn't the problem," he says so quietly, I question if I heard him right.

"Why are you here?" I ask, hands on my hips.

"To talk."

"So, you busted my door down?"

He scoffs as he steps fully into my house, closing the door behind him. "Didn't bust nothing. I used a key."

"Why do you have a key?"

He tosses it to me. "It's the spare from under your mat. Get a better hiding spot."

All I can do is stare as he moves past me into the living room, sinking down into the center of our small couch. With his legs spread wide and his arms draped across the back cushions, he looks like a regal king, one I'd be all too willing to worship—you know, if I didn't kind of want to stab him.

"You're insane."

"Be that as it may, you need a dose of reality, and I'm here to deliver it. Now, have a seat."

"Where would you have me sit?" My eyes flare wide as I look around the room, not even remotely considering my dad's chair as a viable option. "You're taking up the whole damn couch."

Mateo glances from me to the chair before shrugging. "I don't care where you sit, so long as you do it."

I'm not sure why, but I want to push his buttons the same way he's pushing mine. Tit for tat.

I step up to him boldly, even though I'm bluffing. "Your lap looks mighty comfy." I expect him to get a clue and make room for me.

He doesn't.

Instead, he leans forward, wraps an arm around my waist, and pulls, landing me squarely in his lap. I'm momentarily stunned. He's so warm and firm beneath me, it's a fight not to melt right into him and purr like a kitten.

A fight I'm apparently losing, judging by the smugly satisfied rumble coming from Mateo.

For a minute or two, neither of us speak. And while I'd never outwardly admit it, here in his arms with my head pressed to his chest, I feel a sense of peace I haven't felt since my dad passed.

Until he speaks and ruins it.

"We need to talk."

I sigh and pull away from his warmth. "About what? What could we possibly have to discuss?"

"What are you doing, Seraphine?"

"What do you mean? Currently I'm trying to figure out who you think you are!"

"I think I'm someone who cares. I'm someone who is worried about you. Simon told me you haven't been back to work since your dad died. It's been almost a month."

I try to move off of him, but Mateo holds me in place.

"I don't see how it's any of your business."

He brings his lips to my ear. "You're right, it's probably not my business." My stupid, hormone-fueled, traitorous body turns to jelly, imagining him whispering sweet nothings instead. "But I'm going to make it my business."

"Why?" I ask, my voice so thin it borders on whiny.

"Because I know how it feels to lose someone. I know how hard it is to pull yourself out of that deep, dark hole. I've been there, and if it weren't for Desi, I'd have let it swallow me up. I don't want that for you. Your friends don't either, but they're all too worried about overstepping."

I pull back as far as he'll allow and glance at him over my shoulder. "And you're not?"

His sinful lips tilt up in a grin. "Not even a little."

"Why?"

"I've got no skin in the game. Everyone else is walking on eggshells around you. But me? I'm gonna be like a bull in a china shop. You want to cry and hide and let life pass you by. That shit won't fly with me."

He sounds so genuine—but something prickles, like there's more to it. I can't help but feel he has other motives, but at this point, I know I need the help, so I'll take it.

"Okay," I whisper.

"Okay? As in no more bullshit? You've got to get yourself together."

I nod.

"Even if it hurts?" he asks.

"Yeah, even if it hurts."

8

MATEO

I'VE SPENT THE LAST SEVEN DAYS WORKING ON A PLAN FOR Seraphine. A plan her gorgeous, stubborn ass will probably shoot down out of pride alone. The headstrong woman needs help, knows she needs it, and still wants to go it alone.

She's as confounding as she is tempting.

Still, she needs someone to guide her through her grief, and apparently that someone is me. Not that I mind. I'd rather put in the work than watch her waste her potential.

"Alexa—call Seraphine," I command as I turn onto her street. Yesterday I told her I was taking her to lunch. She agreed—reluctantly—so I wouldn't put it past her to try to bail.

The line rings three times before she answers, mumbling a sleepy-sounding hello.

"I'll be there in about two minutes. Be ready."

"What?" she asks, some of the grogginess leaving her tone.

"You heard me." I disconnect the call before she can give me any lip. Sometimes, I think she talks back and picks fights just for the hell of it.

I idle in her driveway, waiting to see if she's going to make me come in and physically get her. A thrill races through me at the thought of tossing her lithe body over my shoulder, my palm pressed tightly against her biteable ass to keep her still as I carry her out to my truck.

Maybe she'd squirm in my grip, mouth off a little, and I'd spank her pretty little ass red. The thought alone has my cock pushing against the zipper of my jeans. Seraphine is a five-alarm fire, and even though I know it'll burn, she's tempting enough for me to willingly stick my hand in the fire.

My budding fantasy fizzles when moments later, Seraphine walks out of the house dressed in a pair of ratty denim cut-offs, a distressed white T-shirt knotted at her waist, a leather jacket, and a pair of knee-high boots.

She looks damn fine. I'm talking I-wouldn't-mind-seeing-her-handprints-on-my-hood fine—which truly says something, because my vehicles are my church.

If only I could do more than look. But I won't—not today, not ever. I won't dishonor my friendship with her father in that way. Also, I highly doubt she's stepmother-material.

She flings open the passenger door and climbs into my truck with a snarl. "You rang?"

"You get an A-plus for following instructions." I throw the truck into reverse. "But an F for attitude."

"So funny I forgot to laugh."

"You seem to forget a lot of things, *mariposita*."

"Where are we going?"

Instead of answering right away, I let her sweat it out a little. From the corner of my eye, I catch her eyes trailing over the ink decorating my arm. I only got it last year, after a lot of waffling back and forth. The way she's biting on her lip says she likes what she sees and it strokes my ego, so I give it a little flex just in case.

"I hate surprises, Mateo. The last one involved a suicide note." Her words are coated in a heartrending mixture of sadness and bitterness, and I instantly feel like an asshole.

I rattle off a string of self-deprecating curses in Spanish. Truly, how could I be so stupid and insensitive? I know I vowed tough love—but that doesn't mean without kindness.

"I'm sorry, Seraphine. Truly."

She shrugs, and I worry I've fucked it all up before even laying my plan out.

"I figured we could go to Buster's. Get some wings and talk. Is that okay?" I'm fully prepared for her to say no, which is why I'm surprised when she murmurs her consent.

"I guess."

"Perfecto."

Ten minutes later, we're tucked into a two-seater booth near the bar, menus in hand.

"Hey there, my name's Kasey and I'll be—" She pauses abruptly when Seraphine looks up toward her. "Oh, hey."

"Hey there, home wrecker."

If it weren't for their matching smiles, I'd be worried about our meals coming with a side of saliva.

"Is that ever gonna get old? It's been like two years!"

Seraphine taps her chin, pretending to mull over the other woman's question. "Mmm… no."

"Whatever. What can I get y'all to drink?" Kasey jots down our orders and scampers off, leaving me to ask Seraphine what exactly their history is.

"Ha!" She snorts out a laugh. "Well… before Drake and Azalea got their shit together, he took Kasey out. He couldn't get over Azalea, though. So, like the shit-for-brains man he is, Drake decided to try and use Kasey to make her jealous. It was a whole thing."

"Uh huh," is all I can say while keeping a straight face. It's times like these that really highlight the age gap between us. She's still elbow-deep in drama, and I'm… not.

"What?" She shrugs one delicate shoulder. "Those two were messy until they made it official."

Kasey returns with our drinks and takes our food order—wings for me, a burger for Seraphine. Before I can fully weigh the consequences of my words, I turn to Seraphine and blurt, "You're a little messy right now, too."

I brace for impact, expecting her to fly off the handle. Instead, I'm met with a single arched brow and soft but lethal words. "Really? You think so?"

Like every man before who's made a shitty comment without thought, I give her the age-old excuse of, "That came out wrong."

Which makes me feel like a jackass, especially when she calmly leans back into her seat and says, "I'm sure it did."

She stares me down as I struggle to find the right words. After a few painfully long seconds tick by, she gets tired of waiting. "Well, go ahead, try again."

Dios mio, this woman. She wants to play hardball, so we will—even if it hurts. "No, you know what? I did mean it."

Her brown eyes widen in disbelief.

"Could I have said it nicer? Definitely, but my poor delivery doesn't change the facts. You're letting your grief rule you." She wants to deny it, to tell me I'm wrong. I can see it in her eyes, but I press ahead. "It ends today, *mariposita.*"

I can tell she's gearing up to tell me off, but Kasey arrives with our food before she can. *Thank God; maybe after she eats, she'll be more receptive to my plan.*

Our heated conversation pauses as we dig into our meals. The fragile silent truce stays in place until the bill is settled and we're in my truck. But as soon as I shift into gear, all bets are off, and Seraphine's ready for war.

"Just who are you to tell me how to run my life?"

"Someone needs to. You're running it into the ground."

She glares. "Be that as it may, it's *my* life. I can do whatever I want with it."

My shoulders shake with silent laughter.

"What?" she snarls.

"You sound like a child. Just because you *can* do something doesn't mean you *should.*" I turn onto the road her dad's shop is on and gun it. Seraphine squeals as I slam on the brakes, bringing us to a jarring stop.

"What the fuck?" she hisses.

"No one else was on the road," I say.

"There's a speed limit for a reason, jackass."

"But my truck can go fast, so..." I'm waiting for her to get my point, and judging from the way she huffs and throws herself back into the seat, she got it—loud and clear.

"Whatever. Why are we here?" The tremble in her voice doesn't escape my notice. I know exactly how hard this is for her—I've been here before and wouldn't wish this on anyone. Regardless, it has to be done.

"Figured we could ride out and check on everything, maybe make some decisions regarding your dad's shop."

"Do we have to?" She fidgets in her seat, looking every bit as pained as I feel.

I pull to a stop in front of the garage bays. "We're already here; might as well." The steadiness of my voice covers the wretchedness working its way through me. While I want to help her, and know she needs to do this, causing her even an iota of pain was not on my to-do list.

She unbuckles and throws open her door. "Fine."

I follow behind her, waiting quietly while she fishes the key out of her purse. I knew coming here was going to be hard, but it may be more so than I anticipated. This shop is her dad's life's work. She practically grew up here. Seraphine was her dad's pride and joy, but these cars, this business, it was his passion. One I know he passed onto her.

Even if she doesn't openly show it, this big metal building means as much to her as it did to him.

Once inside, Seraphine hesitates. I don't rush her. If she needs to stand in the pitch-black dark and gather herself, then that's what we'll do.

I can vividly recall how hard it was to sift through Imani's things—especially her art studio. It was gut-wrenching to sell the space, to sell her pieces; it felt like I was giving little bits of her soul to the highest bidder.

Right as my eyes finally adjust to the dark, she flips the switch for the lights, nearly blinding us both. Bright fluorescent bulbs illuminate the garage, bathing the space in light. We're both quiet at the sight before us.

Everything remains untouched. Tools are littered about, there's a car on the lift, and at least two cars mid-restoration. It's as though Dave went out for lunch and never returned.

I place a hand on the middle of her back, rubbing soothing circles. "It's okay to cry, *mariposita.*"

No sooner than the words leave my lips, she's full-out bawling.

"C'mere." I spin her to face me and wrap my arms around her, pulling her into my chest. I rock us both back and forth, murmuring words of comfort as she lets it all out.

It probably makes me twisted, but some macho part of me wants to roar in triumph over the way she's willing to be vulnerable with me. Seraphine's this fascinating mixture of weakness and strength. She's fragile, yet made of steel. She's broken, yet a warrior—even if she doesn't yet know it.

God knows how long passes before her tears dry and she pulls away from me. "I'm so sorr—" she starts, but I cut her off.

"Do not apologize. This place is sacred to you and visiting it is hard."

She sniffles as she nods. "Honestly, it's surreal to be here. It literally looks like he left in the middle of the day —except instead of coming back, he…" She trails off as a fresh round of tears start.

"Why, Mateo? Why did he leave?"

I pull her back into my arms and press my lips to her temple. The move's as instinctual as breathing. "Shh, *mariposita*. He didn't want to leave you."

"He clearly did," she insists.

I spy a workbench and guide us to it, settling her in my lap. "You know deep down that's not true. Your dad loved you. More than anything else, he loved *you*."

"Then why did he leave?"

A million different answers race through my brain. People are always so quick to call those who end their own lives selfish, even though it's rarely the case.

"Honestly? We may never know. But him ending his life in no way negates his love for you. You hung the moon for that man, Seraphine. I can't begin to understand how alone and betrayed you must feel, but please don't doubt your father's love for you."

She sighs and lays her head back against my chest. "It's hard, though. Why would he leave if he loved me?"

"I can't answer that. But I think... it was more about him than it ever was you."

"You think so?"

"I really do."

She shrugs noncommittally before shrugging out of my embrace and standing. "Everything's the exact same," she murmurs, "and yet totally different."

I rise and follow behind her as she walks over to a jaw-dropping 1970 Plymouth Barracuda. The beast of a ride caught my eye the minute the lights came on, but it wasn't the time.

She approaches it as if it's a wild animal, cautious but curious. She circles it before trailing her fingers reverently over the trim.

"When did he get her?" I ask, tipping my chin toward the partially restored masterpiece.

"He's had her for a while. Just got too sick to work on her."

I drag my eyes over the fine lines of the body, loving every bit of it. She needs work, but she's still a damn fine ride. "Damn."

She shrugs as her gaze hones in on mine. Judging from the fierce look, she's done reminiscing and ready to get down to business. "Why are we here?"

If she's ready to do this, so am I. "We're here because you need to figure out what you want to do with this place."

Ignoring me, or maybe contemplating my words, Seraphine walks along the edges of the garage, taking in every inch of space.

She stops by every stall, every workstation, until she ends her circuit on the opposite side of the 'Cuda from where she started. A frown mars her pretty features. "I don't know, Mateo."

Now's the time to go for broke. *Please let her have an open mind.* "Sell it to me," I say, leveling her with a pleading look over the hood of the 'Cuda.

"Sell what?"

"All of this." I throw my arms out wide. "The shop, the tools, the unfinished projects."

She shakes her head, her previously down-turned lips now twisted up in a snarl. "No! No way. This is my dad's legacy."

I scoff in disbelief as I look around the space. "If you

ignore it any longer, you'll make a mockery of all his hard work, of his reputation, of his *legacy*."

Seraphine lunges for me over the hood of the car, her palm splayed wide, itching to make contact with my cheek.

"Do not," I growl, catching her wrist before she can connect. "*Ever* try to hit me."

Tensions run high as she tries to free herself from my grip, but I tug her closer, causing her to lean fully over the hood. The position puts her luscious cleavage on display; it's a fight to keep my eyes on hers, but now is not the time to check her out.

"Or what?" Her eyes harden as she glares at me, a defiant tilt to her chin. Seraphine wants her words to have bite, but right now, she is all bark.

"*Estás muy malcriada*," I mutter under my breath, which only serves to anger the little spitfire more.

"Excuse me? What did you just say?"

"I said you're acting spoiled." I drag my eyes over her as she tugs against my hold. "Like a child who did not get her way." I release her wrist and round the hood of the car.

"I'm a grown-ass woman!" Seraphine fires back, all but stomping her foot.

"Then act like it!" I roar, advancing her until her back is pressed into the side of the car.

As I stare down at this fragile, broken girl, a grotesque mix of pity and hunger gnaws at me. Of the two, pity is safer; it is the only one I am willing to give any time to, because the hunger is a can of worms I have no intention of opening—ever.

"You claim you're grown; you claim you want to honor

your father's legacy. You lie. You're nothing but a scared, sad child, determined to run all you love into the ground."

She sniffles, and my heart pinches. "I don't want to be…"

Her soft, broken words turn the pinch into a pull. The kind of pull that leads experienced sailors to the depths, to their deaths. The kind of pull that inspires sonnets and songs and movies. The kind of pull I'm helpless to resist.

I skim the back of my hand over her tear-dampened cheek, wiping away the physical evidence of her sorrow. "Then don't be, *mariposita*."

She blinks her big brown eyes up at me. "H-how? How can I not be? I know you're right. I'm ruining everything."

The urge to trade my jeans and T-shirt for armor is strong as I pull her into a hug. "Let me help you. Let me buy this from you; I'm sure you could use the cash. I'll keep your dad's legacy intact." I step back from her, looking down to gauge her reaction.

While her eyes are still watery, there's a determined furrow in her brow. "On one condition," she says, her tone daring me to deny her.

"What's that?"

"Hire me."

SERAPHINE

"Just go inside," I mutter to myself as I pace back and forth on the sidewalk, passing the salon by for the fourth time. "They know you're coming, woman up and go in!"

Even after my paltry pep-talk, I'm no closer to actually going in. "Why is this so hard?"

A bead of sweat rolls down my spine, and my skin feels too tight. The mere thought of facing the women I've called my best friends—my *only* friends—for years has me ready to run home and never leave the safety of my bed ever again.

My stomach churns and my heart races as I finally gather the courage to approach the door. I reach for the handle—*I can do this*. Except before I can make contact, the salon door flies open and I yank my hand away, cradling it to my chest as though I touched a flame.

"Are you going to come in or keep pacing?" Azalea asks bluntly, morphing my anxiety to humiliation.

I shake my head and take a step back. My eyes burn

with unshed tears, but my voice comes out mostly steady. "This was a bad idea."

Azalea cocks her head to the side and steps fully out of the salon, allowing the door to close behind her. "Seraphine, what are you doing?"

"Nothing," I whisper, meaning it in more ways than one. "I'm just gonna—"

"Come inside and spill your guts?" Azalea links her arm with mine and escorts me into the salon. "Perfect idea!"

I slap a smile on my face and hope it looks more natural than it feels.

"Lookie who I found," Azalea announces as we step onto the cutting floor.

"Hey, stranger!" Myla Rose sets her comb and shears down and rushes over to hug me. I study her when she pulls away; her eyes and smile are both wide and honest— she's truly happy to see me.

This little kernel of knowledge loosens the knot in my chest a little.

"Hey, Myles." I keep my voice soft. I feel like an outsider in a salon I worked in for years, and while I know it's my doing, I don't like the way I feel like a visitor in such a familiar place, especially one that once was an escape from all that was happening with Dad over the years. But now, in the wake of his death, it almost feels tarnished.

"We've missed you, you know?" she asks, hugging me again before picking up her comb and shears and resuming her haircut.

"I've missed y'all, too." I keep my eyes downcast, trying to gather some of the fire I used to possess. These days, it seems only a certain hot-bodied mechanic can coax it out of me.

"Could've fooled—*oof!* Ouch!"

I look up in time to see Azalea rubbing her side. My best guess is Myla Rose elbowed her—the thought makes me grin. She's a feisty little redhead, so I wouldn't put bodily harm past her.

"Where's Magnolia?" I ask, wrapping my arms around my midsection.

"She ran over to Dream Beans with Callista for a coffee run."

"Who's Callista?"

Myla Rose and Azalea exchange worried glances.

"Our receptionist," Myles says slowly.

I try to swallow, but there's a golf-ball sized lump in my throat preventing me from doing so. Instead, I nod and try not to cry. I knew they would replace me. I all but forced them to when I ghosted them. I should count myself lucky they're all still willing to speak to me. I know all of this, but still, it stings.

The bell over the door rings, and my cousin walks in along with a beautiful woman who must be Callista. With flawless skin, chestnut hair, and big brown eyes—she's stunning. And judging by the cheek-splitting smile she's rocking, she's nice, too.

Good, I think, nodding to myself. My girls need someone good, and if she's it and they like her, then I do, too.

"Seraphine!" Magnolia squeals when she sees me. It's so out of character for my soft, quiet cousin who hates loud noises that it completely catches me off guard. Even more so when she shoves her coffees into Azalea's hands and runs over to me and wraps me in a tight embrace. "Oh my God, I've missed you!"

Once my stupor wears off, I return her embrace, holding the only family I have left on this earth tightly to me.

By the time we let go, we're both teary-eyed and sniffling.

"You're really here." Her voice is tinged with a hint of awe.

"I am."

"I haven't heard your voice, seen your face, nothing in more than a month."

"I know." Worry lands in my gut like a lead weight. *Is she angry with me? Will she ask me to leave? Maybe she doesn't really want me here?*

I lock my hands behind me and take a small step backward. My breathing accelerates as every imaginable worst-case scenario presents itself to me. I'm on the verge of bolting when Callista walks over to me.

"You must be Seraphine."

I breathe in deeply and exhale before lifting my eyes to hers. "Yes." My voice is barely audible.

"You've left me some mighty big shoes to fill. These ladies love you fierce."

A smile works its way free at her words. *How is it this stranger knew exactly what I needed to hear?* "I love them, too." This time my words are clear.

"I'm Callista." She extends her hand toward me, and I shake it.

"It's really nice to meet you," I say, surprised by how much I mean it.

With our introductions out of the way, Magnolia

passes me one of the many cups she and Callista returned with. I take a long pull from the straw, letting my taste-buds revel in the cool, toffee-coffee goodness.

Myla Rose finishes up her client and flips the sign to "closed" once she leaves. "Now, let's talk about what you've been up to."

Azalea smirks. "You know, other than ghosting us."

Guilt prickles again, but I push it to the back burner and fill my friends in on the disaster-zone that is my life.

"Uh, well, I sold Dad's shop."

"What? Why? To who?" Myla Rose demands, rapid-fire.

"It's a long story." I fidget in my seat under the weight of their stares. "But Mateo bought it."

"Reyes? Mateo Reyes?" Magnolia asks.

"Yup. And he hired me, to you know, help out and stuff."

"And stuff, huh?" Azalea asks as she wags her brows, infusing the moment with some much-needed humor.

We talk a little more, and I learn Callista recently moved to Dogwood for a fresh start. She's a single mom to toddler-aged twins, a recent divorcee, and was in the middle of cosmetology school when her ex-husband walked out. So she's basically perfect for them.

Once all of our catching up is out of the way, Magnolia guides me to her chair. "What are we doing with your hair?"

I shrug and give her carte blanche. Four hours later, I walk out with subtle caramel highlights and about six inches off the ends, leaving it level with my breasts.

They say a woman who cuts her hair is about to change her life—here's to hoping like hell that's true.

MATEO

"ARE WE REALLY GOING TO KEEP DOING THIS?" SERAPHINE asks, wiping the sweat from her brow while simultaneously trying to kill me with her glare alone.

"*Sí*." I lean back against the steel cabinet.

She's so over my little quizzes that she's practically snarling at me. But I don't care. I need to know if she grew up around cars, or if she actually *knows* cars before we open and I truly put her to work.

Which is why ten of the last fourteen days have been spent cataloging every item in the garage to get ready for the relaunch. I won't lie—she seems to know her stuff. But I need to be sure before I turn her loose in here.

"Fine," she grits out, nodding her head toward her dad's—I mean *my*—'Cuda. "That beautiful beast is one of only six-hundred-and-fifty-two produced that year. It's got a 440-six pack with an aluminum Edelbrock manifold topped by three 2300 series carb. A lot of people wanted the 426 Hemi, but the automatic 440 was actually faster."

Seraphine shrugs like she didn't just make my dick

hard spouting off classic car facts like some kind of sexy, tan-skinned encyclopedia. A groan rumbles up from my chest as I stare at her. She's dressed down in those godforsaken bootie shorts and a hoodie—and yet, the combo is hotter than any lingerie on the market. She's a clueless seductress—tempting me without even meaning to.

"Anything else you want, *sir?*" The little bite of sass she adds at the end of her sentence only makes me want her more. She's young and wild and bratty, and I'd love nothing more than to take her over my knee and show her exactly what else I want.

"No, you're good."

"Great." She flips her head forward and gathers her hair into a messy ponytail and secures it with an elastic from her wrist before plopping down onto the bench. "When are we opening to the public?"

I cross the shop and take a seat next to her. "I'd say we got about two weeks left on the reno, then soft launch for the mechanical side of things and maybe a month on the resto."

"Reno?" She whips her entire body around to face me so that she's straddling the bench. "How could you? You're just going to destroy—we never talked about a renovation!"

"Calm down, *mariposita.*"

After those two dreaded words, Seraphine's practically shooting laser beams out of her eyes. "Adding that stupid nickname doesn't negate you telling me to calm down, asshole."

I can't help but grin at her self-righteous anger. "I know there is a lot of sentimental value here for you. I need you to trust me to do what is best for the business in a way that will still honor your father. He worked hard and was good at his craft. I do not wish to erase that. I merely want to bring the shop up to date, okay?"

Looking properly chastised, she nods and whispers, "Okay."

"Yeah?"

"Yeah." She nibbles on her lip. "I trust you."

The way her moods yo-yo is enough to make me feel dizzy, but I know it's because she's still hurting—that the loss of her father is still a raw, gaping wound. She needs to heal, and I am determined to help her.

Even if that means letting her lash out from time to time. Better to use me as an outlet than popping off at some unsuspecting stranger.

I know that's not exactly healthy, but grief is a strange beast, and I know this soul-crippling sadness of hers is only a season. Eventually her storm cloud tears will give way to sunny smiles, and I damn sure intend to be around to see them.

"Tell you what—why don't you help out with it?"

Her nose crinkles. "With the reno?"

I nod. "Yeah, we start tomorrow. Be here at seven o'clock sharp."

"Do I have to?" she whines and gives me puppy dog eyes.

"*Sí.*"

She pouts, and it takes my all not to grab her by her hoodie and yank her down the bench to me so I can kiss the frown right off her lips.

I settle for leaning into her space as I stand, loving how she smells like lavender and motor oil. *Who knew the combination would be so sexy?*

"Fine, I'll be here."

"I know." I offer her my most winning smile and extend a hand down to help her up.

She accepts it, grumbling under her breath the entire time.

"Do I need to make sure you're up on time?"

Seraphine crosses her arms over her chest and glares. "We've been over this. I'm grown."

"I know," I say again, keeping to myself that I was hoping she'd say yes. There's something about her raspy morning voice that just does it for me. As sad as it is, I've been going out of my way to hear it.

Desi says I'm *fuera de sí*—out of my mind, when it comes to Seraphine, and while I always tell her she's the crazy one, I'm starting to realize she might be right.

"Mi rey." *Imani runs her fingers over the shaved sides of my hair, tickling my scalp. I shiver at the sensation and lean farther into her touch. "I've been watching you."*

I lean back enough to catch her eyes. "Watching me?"

She nods. "You seem happier."

"I'm always happy with you."

She shakes her head; her beautiful corkscrew curls sway with the movement. "You're not with me, not really."

I try to protest, but she presses a finger to my lips and shushes me.

"In spirit, yes. In heart, always." Her lips tip up in a tender smile. "She's good for you—and my pollito.*"*

"Who?" I rack my brain, trying to figure out who she could

mean. There's no one—and I mean not one single person—who could ever replace her.

"You know," she says cryptically.

I adamantly shake my head. "I do not know. You are my only reina—my *queen."*

Imani smiles her secret smile; the one reserved for when she knows something I don't and she can't wait for it to smack me upside the back of my head.

"You don't need another queen," she murmurs. Finally agreeing with me. "But perhaps a butterfly..."

The vision of my wife wavers, her rich brown skin and radiant smile flickers in and out twice before she blows me a kiss and disappears altogether, and countless little butterflies take her place, fluttering all around me.

I call after her, begging her to come back, to explain. "Trust your heart, my king," comes her disembodied voice. "For I am there and will never lead you astray."

"Imani!" I shout, causing all but one of the delicate winged creatures to scatter. It flaps its intricately designed wings twice before landing on my arm.

I look down at it, but the deeper meaning sits just beyond my reach.

"Imani?" I ask one more time.

Her tinkling laughter is my only reply, and all too quickly it merges with the sound of my alarm clock.

I bolt upright in bed, trying to recall the details of my dream. But it's no use. With the morning sunlight seeping in through my blinds, only fragments remain.

"Dad!" Desi yells from the hall outside my closed bedroom door "Dad! Get up! It's already six-thirty!"

"Fuck," I grumble under my breath, frustrated as hell

over the bits and pieces I can remember from my weird dream.

"Heard that," comes from the other side of my door.

"Give me fifteen and I'll be ready."

"I'll start a pot of coffee."

I grin to myself as I toss off the covers and head to my bathroom, wondering how I got so lucky to have such a good kid.

After a quick shower and shave, I dress in a pair of coveralls, shove my feet into my boots, and head to the kitchen in search of coffee.

"Good morning," Desi chirps. She's sitting on the countertop, dressed in her own version of work clothes, sipping coffee from a pink mug that used to be her mother's.

"Why are you so chipper?" I pour myself a thermos of coffee, knowing I'll have to take it with me if I want to get enough down to feel its effects.

"Am I not allowed to be happy, Dad?"

I flick her shoulder. "I don't ever want you to be anything other than happy, *pollito*."

She rolls her eyes. "Such a sap. C'mon, let's go. We can grab some kolaches for everyone on the way!"

I quirk a brow. "Everyone who?"

"Well…" She drains the contents of her mug, hops down, and places it in the sink. "I know you asked Seraphine to lend a hand. And I might have asked Uncle Arrón and Aunt Silvi to come, too."

I massage my temples in anticipation of the headaches I know I'll have by the end of the day.

"Are you mad?" Desi's shoulders slump. "You're mad."

"I'm not," I assure her. "Thank you for calling in reinforcements. I guess we better get those kolaches, because that's the only payment they're getting."

She laughs, and I grab the keys to my GTO.

"Can I drive?"

"Sure." I pointedly swap the GTO keys for the keys to the truck. Both cars are expertly restored, but parts for the truck are easier to come by, so if she dings it, fixing it won't be a total nightmare.

She pouts, but it doesn't sway me. "The truck or bust, kid."

"Fine." She climbs into the driver's seat and cranks the engine. "Let's go!"

Twenty minutes later, Desi whips my precious truck into one of the few parking spaces in front of the garage. "Easy, Des! Easy."

"Chill, old man. I am a perfect driver."

"You are a menace to everyone on the road." I'm lying; the kid is a great driver, but I can't have that knowledge inflating her already oversized teenage head.

"Your criticisms are nothing more than a reflection of yourself."

"Say what?" I cock my head to the side as I look at her.

Desi shrugs and kills the engine. "I'm just saying, you taught me everything I know."

"You little shit!" I reach over the console and ruffle her hair, knowing sure-fire it'll rile her up. She's got her mama's curls, and at sixteen, her hair is off-limits.

"Oh my God, stop!" She bats my hand away, laughing. "It's gonna frizz!"

"Who cares, *pollito*? It's just hair."

"Easy for you to say—you're gonna be bald in like a decade!"

"It's on now!" I lunge for her hair again, but she scrambles out of the truck and hightails it into the safety of the garage.

I flip down the visor and check my hairline in the mirror. I know she was only trying to rile me up, and like the sucker I am, I played right into her plans.

After I pull the keys from the ignition and pocket them, I grab the box of still warm kolaches and head inside.

The sound of boisterous laughter greets me as I enter the building. Somehow, in the two minutes it took me to get inside, Desi, Arrón, and Silvi are playing some deranged version of hide-and-seek, while Seraphine hovers near the coffeepot, looking uncomfortable in her own skin.

Her pinched brow and hunched shoulders light up every protective nerve in me. I don't like seeing my girl look so miserable in a place that should bring her peace.

Fuck—did I just call her my girl?

The revelation has me ready to turn around and run back to the truck. But I've never once hidden from a problem, and I don't intend to start now. So what if my body yearns for her—craves her even. I am a grown-ass man who knows impulse control.

I can *want* all I want, as long as I don't *act*.

Of their own volition, my feet carry me toward her. "Are you hungry, *mariposita?*" I ask, my voice low.

She glances up at me from beneath her sooty lashes and licks her lips. "I could eat."

Dios mio, this woman! I hold the box out in front of me, as an offering and a barrier. "Kolache?"

She pops the top and moans as the smell of smoked

sausage wafts upward. *Camshaft, rocker arm, hydraulic adjuster, intake valve...* I start calling engine parts in my head, in a desperate effort to hang on to the impulse control I was just patting myself on the back for.

"Exhaust valve and piston. Mateo, are you quizzing me again? Do I need to name some more parts to earn my breakfast?"

"Didn't realize I was speaking aloud," I grind out the words, caught between arousal and embarrassment. "Please, just take one."

Seraphine gives me a questioning look before shrugging and grabbing a kolache. She takes a bite and does this happy little wiggle as she groans. "So good! Should I make some coffee?"

I glance past her to the old Bunn coffee machine. "Does that dinosaur still work?"

"That coffee maker has been in this exact spot since before I was born. It will probably survive the end of the world."

We share a private laugh. There was a reason Dave restored his projects to period—he liked the past and largely lived in it. God knows, this shop is a testament to that.

"You gonna share the wealth?" Arrón yells, breaking up our moment.

Seraphine smiles and shoos me away, looking determined to get that Bunn up and running. Now if only I can get her determined to attack life in the same way.

SERAPHINE

Mateo lingers for a moment after his brother calls out to him. He runs his deep brown eyes over my body, warming me from the inside. The way his lips quirk up makes me think he likes what he sees, which is something I am not ready to think about, even if I did pick this outfit with him in mind.

Though, if I had known his family and daughter would be here with us, I'd have probably gone with something a little more modest. Not that there's anything wrong with my cut-offs and loose-fitting crop top. They're comfy, and I don't mind them getting dirty, but still, I feel like I have a flashing neon sign over my head that reads *desperate.*

So, I turn away and start a pot of coffee.

My reprieve doesn't last long, thanks to this dinosaur's crazy-fast brew time, and before I know it, the entire Reyes clan is surrounding me, all vying for a cup of joe.

"First cup!" Arrón hollers.

But his sister—who I've yet to be formally introduced to—knocks him out of the way. "Brains before beauty."

The younger Reyes brother waggles his brows. "So, you admit I'm prettier than you, Silvi?"

"Oldest and wisest goes first," Mateo says.

Desi worms her way to the front. "Pretty sure it's women and children first—both of which I am, so scoot back, losers."

I can't help but smile at their antics. You can tell they're a close-knit family with a lot of love between them.

"Everyone knows the brewer gets first dibs." The words fall from my lips without much thought, as if bantering with them is something I've been doing all my life.

"She's got a point," Arrón concedes, but Mateo clutches his heart like I've fatally wounded him. "*Mariposita,* why you gotta do me so wrong? I even brought you breakfast!"

Laughter spills from my lips as I pour myself a cup of caffeinated nectar. "For that little guilt trip, you can go last."

Desi and Arrón crack up, while Silvi glances between her oldest brother and me, a small smirk playing on her lips.

"You wound me," Mateo declares while hauling himself to the back of the line.

"Your ego can handle it," Desi shoots back as I pour her a mug.

"Watch it, *pollito*, or you might end up grounded."

Desi laughs, knowing her dad is full of hot air, but Silvi rushes to her defense. "You can't ground my niece for teasing you. I will not allow it."

Mateo reaches around Arrón and tugs on the end of

his sister's ponytail. "Oh, yeah? How are you gonna stop me?"

Silvi's brown eyes twinkle with mirth. "Mamá."

"You wouldn't!"

The youngest Reyes sibling grins, looking every bit like a mischievous little sister. "Bet." She and Desi bump hips and knock their mugs together before making room for Arrón.

"You know she would, Mate. Remember when we wouldn't let her come to the ballpark with us, so she threw a baseball at the television and told *Jefecita* it was us?"

Mateo barks out a laugh from deep in his belly. "Devious little shit. *Mujer diabólica.*"

"Did you just call me a devil woman?" his sister asks. Her voice is hard but she's smiling.

"Damn straight." He takes the mug I offer him and winks. "Now, put away your pitchfork and grab a paintbrush."

I collect all of the mugs while the guys get the paint ready. I'm halfway through washing them when I feel someone watching me.

"Oh, hey," I turn, surprised to see Silvi standing there. At about five foot, she's petite but with attitude in spades. Her skin is a flawless golden-tan and her black hair, though tied up in a ponytail, spills down her back.

"We haven't met yet." I can't put my finger on it, but something in her tone makes me feel like I'm being tested —and quite possibly failing.

"Nope, we haven't." *Yep, definitely failing.* "I'm Seraphine." I offer her my hand to shake.

"I'm Silvia, but you can call me Silvi," she says, clasping my hand in hers.

"I've heard a lot about you," I blurt out, for lack of anything better to say.

She fluffs her ponytail. "And I you."

The thought of Mateo—or even Desi—talking about me has me feeling like I'm about to take flight.

"Oh, uh, really?"

"Really. You seem to make them happy."

I blink twice. "It's not—we're not—"

"Not yet." She mutters something under her breath in Spanish. "You're both too bone-headed to see what is right in front of you."

The heat radiating in my cheeks threatens to burn me from the inside out. "Really, you have the wrong idea about us. Your brother... he's... my friend?"

Silvi laughs. "You say that like it is a question."

"It kind of is," I whisper.

"You are his and he is yours. You'll see." She leans in closer. "But know this, if you hurt my brother or my niece, I won't hesitate to crush your wings, little butterfly."

I gulp and manage to stutter out some sort of reply. Judging from her pleased smile, it must have been what she wanted to hear.

"Great. Good talk." She turns away from me, but pauses a few steps away and adds, "Maybe we can grab lunch one day?"

Stunned stupid, all I can manage is a nod.

Four hours later, it's just Mateo, Desi, and me. His sister left two hours in to help their mother with something, and Arrón dipped out shortly after to head over to their other shop.

"It looks good, right?" Mateo says, his voice full of pride at our paint job. Every wall in the shop is painted a perfectly neutral gray, save for the back wall, which is a brilliant, bright white.

And while it does look good, I'm thankful he had the good sense to tarp the floor and cover the cabinets and equipment, because there may be more paint on us than the walls.

"It looks great, Dad," Desi agrees, glancing up from her phone screen.

"What's so interesting over there, *pollito*?"

"Meg and Renee want to go to Vinny's for pizza."

Mateo raises a brow.

"And I want to go, too?"

"Then ask me the way you should," he tells his daughter.

"Such a stickler for manners." Desi barely suppresses an eye roll. "Dad, may I please get pizza with my friends?"

"Much better. Keep your phone on and check in?"

"I will." She taps around on her screen, most likely texting. "Oh, but I'll need the truck to go home and shower."

He cringes slightly but tosses her his keys all the same. "Be safe."

She catches the keys and slides them in her front pocket. "I will. Love you."

"Love you, too." He wraps his daughter in a hug and sends her on her way.

"You do realize you just stranded yourself here, right?" I ask, rolling my lips inward to keep from grinning.

"I do now," he sighs. "But you'll help me out, won't you, *mariposita?*"

I massage my ears a few times to clear them before asking him to repeat himself. *Are auditory hallucinations a thing—because his voice sounds chock-full of innuendo.*

He slowly runs his tongue over his lower lip. "I said, you'd help me out."

The words themselves may be innocent, but the way he's saying them is anything but. Which creates a real problem. Do I flirt back and run the risk that I'm imagining his toe-curling tone or do I brush it off?

But what if he is flirting and I ignore it and then he feels rejected and I miss any shot I might ever have with him?

Be bold, a small voice whispers from somewhere in the back of my mind. *Be brave.*

I decide to listen and take a step closer to him. He eyes me hungrily as I lay my hand on his *very* solid chest. "I'll get you anywhere you want to go." My voice has this breathlessness to it that's wholly unfamiliar to me.

Then again—most anything to do with flirting with the opposite gender is foreign to me. But if his dilated pupils are anything to go by, maybe I'm not a complete failure.

Mateo wraps an arm around my middle and pulls me to him, skimming his nose from my temple down to my ear. He groans softly as he inhales. "You are a dangerous woman."

"Are you scared of a little danger?" I whisper,

wondering where the hell these words are even coming from as I rise up onto my tiptoes.

Wordlessly, he leans down and presses his lips to mine. Our mouths fit together like two pieces of a puzzle. Warmth blossoms in my core as he moves his lips over mine, coaxing my mouth open for him to deepen the kiss.

His tongue meets mine ever so briefly before he jerks away from me as though I've burned him.

"We can't," is all he says before he turns and walks away.

Fury and humiliation flow together in my veins, giving way to burning resentment. *Am I a game to him? Is that why he's been so kind? Help the sad, broken girl only to break her a little more? Well, if that's the case, I'll show him.*

With my shoulders rolled back and my head held high, I march past where he's rolling up a section of tarp. He calls my name, but I ignore him. He can fuck right off.

Once I reach the paintbrushes, I bend at the waist, knowing full and well he's being treated to a view. I give my hips a little wiggle as I collect all of the rollers and paintbrushes into a large bucket to my right.

Mateo groans, and I smile. He thought he could toy with me… lead me on. He's about to learn—*payback's a bitch and I'm going to serve it up sexier than ever.*

"Seraphine," he says again, frustration coloring his words as I pass by him again.

I still remain silent. That jackass doesn't deserve my words.

At the sink, I begin rinsing the paint from the brushes, humming softly to keep myself sufficiently distracted.

"Do not ignore me," he says from behind me, close enough I can feel the heat of his body.

Naturally, I do the opposite of his command and pretend he's nothing more than a warm, surly shadow.

"Seraphine," he growls my name before softening his tone. "Please."

"You wanna hit up a drive-thru once we finish cleaning up? I'm starving."

"We need to talk about—"

"I'm thinking chicken tenders." I nod to myself. "Yeah, definitely tenders."

I hear him groan, but I keep my eyes on the task at hand.

"Eres desesperante."

"What was that?" I ask, pretending I didn't hear him versus not having a clue of what he said. From his tone, I think he's annoyed. *Serves him right.*

"You are making me crazy!"

I throw the brush I'm washing down into the sink and whip around to face him. "Oh, *I* make *you* crazy? Pot meet kettle!"

"What?" He glares at me.

"You're the most infuriating man I've ever known. Sometimes I think we're friends. Other times, I think you can barely tolerate me. And then today, you have the audacity to not only kiss me, but to then act like the taste of my lips repulsed you!"

Mateo honest to God growls. "Repulse me? *Mariposita*, I would gladly survive off of your taste alone. I could live and die—happily—with the memory of you pressed against me."

My body practically liquifies at his smooth words. "Then why?"

"You are off-limits. Forbidden."

"What?" Now I'm the one glaring.

"I told myself a long time ago that I could look but never touch. But the more time we spend together, the more my resolve weakens. You are like a witch, casting a spell, luring me to you. Tempting me. Torturing me." He squares his shoulders. "But I will not give in. I will stay strong."

"Okay," I say slowly, nodding, like his words make sense, even though they don't. "But why am I off-limits? We're both adults. We're obviously both interested. I don't see the problem."

He pinches the bridge of his nose. "I wish things were different. Truly, I do."

The back of my eyes sting with the threat of tears. I turn back toward the sink and resume cleaning the brushes and rollers. "So." My voice comes out hoarse. "How about those chicken tenders?"

"Yeah, *mariposita,* that... sounds good."

12

MATEO

OUR LIPS BARELY TOUCHED. AND YET FOR AN ENTIRE WEEK, she's all I've been able to taste. Her scent, her heat, her anger—it's as if all of it has somehow become a tangible thing, content to follow me around and taunt me over what could have been.

It doesn't help that I haven't heard from her since she dropped me off last weekend.

I eye my phone lying on the island and debate reaching for it—I've almost texted her more times than I can count, but outside of confirming plans, we're not really the texting kind of friends.

Still, the way things went down irks me.

How I went from vowing to never act on my lustful feelings for her to shoving my tongue into her mouth is beyond me. Seraphine Reynolds is every single thing I want and nothing I need all tied up in a pretty bow—one I'm itching to untie. Except I know nothing good will come from it. In fact, I'd wager a bet that falling into anything with her would be as catastrophic as opening Pandora's box.

"Dad!" Desi shoulder checks me as she walks past me into the kitchen. "How much longer are you going to do this?"

I sit up a little straighter on my stool. "Do what?"

My daughter waves her hand in the air in my general direction. "This."

"Still not following, Des."

She rolls her eyes in the way only a teenage girl can. "Dad, you know I love you, right?"

I nod.

"Okay, good. Remember that."

Right as I go to ask her what she means, the sound of the doorbell stops me. "Desi, who is here?"

She mumbles under her breath something that sounds a lot like *everyone.*

The sound of chimes fills the house again as our mystery visitor presses the bell again. I shoot my meddling daughter a scathing look before vacating my chair to answer the door.

Sure enough, *everyone* is here. Mamá, Arrón, and Silvi are all packed onto my front porch like sardines. I'm half tempted to close the door and leave them there.

But I would never disrespect my family like that—even if their visit is probably going to end up being some kind of unnecessary, quasi-intervention.

"My son!" my mother cries as she lunges over the threshold to wrap me in a hug. She holds me tight, hugging me as though she hasn't seen me in ages, when it's only been a few days.

I'd be lying, though, if I said it didn't make me feel a

little better. Even as a grown-ass man, sometimes a mother's hug is what you need.

"Now, where is my *pollito?*"

"I'm here," Desi says from behind me, and just like that, I'm chopped liver.

The two of them disappear to God knows where and I turn back to my siblings and sigh. "Come in."

We walk into the kitchen and I offer them a drink. "I've got beer in the fridge, Cokes in the garage, water, juice."

"A Coke sounds good," Arrón says.

Grinning, I nod. "You know where they are."

Silvi laughs. "Aren't you just the host with the most?"

"Technically, *my daughter* is your host," I say, as Desi waltzes into the room, drinks in hand.

"Here's a Dr. Pepper for you," she says, handing my brother a can. "And a Diet Coke for you, Silvi."

"What about me?" I ask teasingly, and without missing a beat she says, "You know where they are."

The heckling is immediate.

"Sick burn!" Arrón hollers, holding his hand out toward Desi for a high-five, while Silvi *boos* loudly and my mother mutters in Spanish.

Even as the butt of the joke, I can't help but smile. There's something about being around family—for me, at least—that always makes me feel better when I'm out of sorts. They're my foundation when I'm weak, my glue when I'm broken, and sometimes, they're a thorn in my side. But I wouldn't trade them for anything.

They heckle me a little more before their laughter tapers off into curiosity.

"Tell me, Mate," my mother says. "Why are we here?" I

can see why she's confused; her house is our usual gathering place.

I shrug and point to my daughter. "Ask her."

All eyes turn to Desi. "You're here today because…" She pauses for dramatic effect, her mouth spreading into what can only be described as an evil grin. "Dad's met someone."

"Whoa!" I shout, but my denial is lost in the fray as my family all demands to know more about my new—*nonexistent*—woman.

"I knew there was something between y'all!" Silvi accuses. "She told me there wasn't, but I knew it!"

"Seraphine?" my brother asks. "About time."

"You'll really like her," Desi says to my mother, but she silences her with a single hard look.

"A woman?" *Mamá* asks. "You have met a woman?"

"No." The word feels like a lie; I shake my head to reinforce it… to make myself believe it.

"Dad!"

"Hush, *pollito*. Your father and I are talking."

Desi huffs and slumps down onto a barstool.

"Why does everyone know this woman but not me? Your brother and sister and even your daughter have met her, but not me? You will bring her to dinner."

"Mam—"

"Your celebratory dinner for the new shop. She will come."

With wide eyes, I look around the room for help. Judging by the matching smirks on Arrón and Silvi's faces, the calvary isn't coming anytime soon.

"Take me home, *hijito*," she says to my brother as she scowls at me. "Suddenly, I'm not up for visiting."

"Are you sure?" Arrón asks.

She nods once. "Yes. And when we get home, I'll make *tacos de barbacoa*."

"Why does he get *barbacoa*?" I squawk, not caring a single iota over how lame I sound. That stuff is delicious, and knowing my brother, he will gloat for days on end about this.

Mamá glares. "Then you shouldn't have lied."

"I didn't lie!"

"A lie by omission is still a lie," Silvi adds unhelpfully.

"I didn't omit anything," I growl. "There's nothing between us!"

"Denial isn't any better, Dad."

"Impossible—you people are impossible." I throw my hands up in defeat. "I'm not looking for a relationship! Especially one with *her*!"

"What's wrong with Seraphine, Dad?" My daughter wears her confusion and hurt as plain as day on her face. "I really like her, and I know you do, too."

"She is too young. Immature. Practically a child." My tone is more abrasive than I mean for it to be. My frustration with the entire situation is morphing; what started as an ember is quickly becoming an inferno.

"*Mijo*." Mamá moves across the room to me and takes my hand in hers. "My son, is her age your only holdup?"

I seesaw my free hand in the space between us. "Eh. Mostly."

"Your father was much older than me. Almost twenty-two years." She squeezes the hand she is still holding. "Search your heart, Mate."

Without a rebuttal in mind, I nod.

"Bring her to dinner," she murmurs as she leans forward to kiss my cheek.

"Wait, you're still leaving?"

She sighs. "You may not have lied to me, but you're lying to yourself, and that may be worse."

Knowing I've already lost the battle, I kiss her cheek as well and resign myself to figuring out how in the hell I'm going to get Seraphine to a family dinner in two days when we're hardly talking. And how I'm going to get Desi to bring me home barbacoa without Mamá catching on.

13

SERAPHINE

"WAIT, WAIT, WAIT. IT WAS A KISS AND A DISS?" AZALEA asks, while absentmindedly running her fingers through her pug Boudreaux's short fur.

I toe the porch swing back, letting the brisk fall air soothe some of the heat scalding my cheeks. We've spent the last hour on Azalea's back porch dissecting the whole kiss thing from last weekend. "Hardly a kiss."

"But your lips touched—Brody! No, don't put leaves in your mouth!" Myla Rose leans over and fishes the debris out of her toddler's mouth with a huff. "We do not eat things off the ground, okay, dude?"

"O'tay, Mama."

She ruffles his curls. "Go play with Willow."

He scampers off, and she turns back to me. "Lip contact?"

I bob my head back and forth. "There was tongue involved"—my friends start to howl— "but only for like a second! I swear, the whole thing was over before it even started."

Azalea squints her eyes at me. "It still counts."

"I really don't think it does. He acted like he was Snow-freaking-White and my mouth was a poisonous apple."

"Oooh, maybe you need to try again, then, and this time he can be the prince instead?"

I roll my eyes at Azzy. God love her. "Pretty sure it doesn't work like that."

She shrugs. "It could. It's your fairy tale, write it the way you want and fuck the rest."

"Shh." Magnolia holds a finger to her lips. "Little ears."

Myla Rose laughs. "Poor Brody hears it enough at home from Cash and Drake."

"What do you think, Mags?" I ask my cousin. "You've been pretty quiet."

She scrunches her face up, tilting her head to one side and then the other. "I think... you're both very much attracted to one another. And while there's obvious chemistry, y'all are scared. Which is understandable. New things can be really scary." She smiles wistfully. "But they can be really awesome, too."

"Plus," Azalea interjects, "he flat-out said he was into you. He called you *forbidden*, and everyone knows forbidden fruit tastes the sweetest."

"I'm not a freaking apple."

"But he wants to take a bite out of you like one!" Azalea smirks like she's bested me.

"He got caught up in the moment. It was nothing—it meant nothing."

Magnolia hums under her breath. "It meant something to you though."

My phone rings before I can reply. My eyes widen when I see Mateo's name flash across the screen.

"Who is it?" Myla asks.

"It's him."

"Answer!" all three women shout.

I slide the bar on the screen to the right and bring the phone to my ear. "Hello?"

"Seraphine, hey." Even through the phone, his deep, lightly accented voice makes me feel all warm and gooey.

Too bad I'm still mad at him. "Did you need something?"

He coughs in disbelief. "No. Well, kind of. Yes."

"Which is it, Mateo?" I make sure to add a little extra bite to my tone, even though I'm secretly loving how flustered he sounds.

"Yes, I need something. I need you to meet me at the garage tomorrow morning."

"Why? We don't open until next Monday."

I can nearly sense his frustration through the phone. "I have something to show you. Please, Seraphine?"

"Yeah, okay. What time?"

"Nine?"

"I'll be there." I end the call and slide my phone into the front pocket of my hoodie.

"Well?" Azalea asks. "What did he say?"

"Nothing really. Told me to meet him at the shop tomorrow morning."

Myla Rose taps her chin. "Did he say why?"

"Nope."

"Well, dress sexy," Azalea says.

"And maybe bring him some coffee?" Magnolia adds.

My lips quirk up into a half-smile. "Hell no; he can bring me coffee."

"'Atta girl!" Myla Rose crows, and the four of us dissolve into laughter.

The following morning, I decide taking both Azalea and Magnolia's advice couldn't hurt. Really, it's a win-win: a kickass outfit to serve as armor and piping hot coffee as a peace offering.

I dress in ripped jeans and a slouchy, cream-colored sweater that hangs off of my left shoulder in a way that's as sexy as it is sweet. I can't resist playing up the sexy just a little though, and layer a mauve lace bralette underneath.

I'm out the door by eight-fifteen, giving myself plenty of time to swing by Dream Beans for coffee. Hopefully Hazel's working—God love her, the girl remembers everyone's orders, which will make my caffeinated bribe a sure thing.

The drive from my house to the coffee shop passes in a blur of nerves. "I am a badass. I am worthy. I am loved," I repeat my little D-I-Y mantra the entire drive until my anxiety settles back down to a dull roar in the recess of my mind.

"Good morning, Seraphine," my favorite barista calls out as soon as I walk through the door. Between that and scoring curbside parking, maybe for what feels like the first time ever, luck is on my side. "You want your usual?"

"Yes, please," I say as I step up to the stunning

reclaimed wood counter. "And whatever Mateo Reyes usually orders as well."

"Hmm." Hazel's eyebrows inch toward her hairline in surprise. "You got it."

She tells me my total and swipes my card before sending me to the end of the counter to wait. Three minutes later, I'm out the door with a beverage in each hand.

I crank my RAV4's radio to max volume for the ride to the shop and sing every song that plays at the top of my lungs. I hit two red lights on the way and add some pretty sweet dance moves at both of them.

I'm sure I look like a fool, but I've found that doing my own version of *Carpool Karaoke* is really soothing when I feel myself spiraling toward a meltdown. I know I should probably talk to an actual therapist instead of spending my free time Googling coping techniques, but so far, they're working.

As the shop comes into view, I have to blink to make sure I'm not seeing things. The once dingy, faded gray building is now an eye-catching combination of charcoal with red accents.

I park the car and spring out, excited to get a better look.

"You like it?" Mateo asks from behind me.

"Where did you come from?" I ask, whirling around to face him, my heart racing a mile a minute at his unexpected appearance.

His brown eyes light with a smile that could rival the sun. "I was sitting in my truck when you drove up." He moves to my side and nods toward the building. "You like?"

I glance up at him. "It's amazing."

"There's more." His fingers brush mine, as if he's going to take my hand, but he slides his hands in his pockets instead. "C'mon."

There's a large something covered by a tarp leaning against the side of the building. "You ready for this?"

"For what?"

"This!" he exclaims, pulling the tarp away.

I can hardly believe what I'm looking at. Tears well up and fall freely as I step forward to get a closer look. "Mateo." My voice wavers as a gamut of emotions slam into me. "You… you did this?"

"*Sí.*"

I run my fingers over the large, round sign. It sports a 1970s GTO over the words *Dave's Garage*. It's everything my dad would have wanted and more.

Still in a state of disbelief, I turn toward him and ask, "You did this for me?"

"Yes."

"Oh my God!" I throw myself into his arms with enough force that he stumbles backward a bit.

"Whoa, *mariposita.*" He reluctantly returns my embrace. "You're happy? You like it?"

"I love it." My words come out muffled since my face is pressed firmly to his chest.

"*Qué bueno,*" he murmurs roughly into my hair.

In this moment, I don't care that I don't know what he said, or that I'm still mad at him. All of that takes a back seat as I sink into him and let the warmth of his body and the steady rhythm of his heart soothe all of my hurts.

It physically pains me to pull away from him, but I do.

"Thank you, Mateo. You have no idea how much this means to me."

"There's one more thing."

"What?" I practically shout my question, because after the new look of the shop and the new sign, I can't wait to see what's next.

"Inside; let's go."

He fishes his keys from his pocket and slides the key into the lock, turns it, and opens the door. I go to move past him, but he lays a hand on my shoulder, halting my progress.

From behind me, he whispers, "Close your eyes."

He's so close to me I can smell his mind-altering scent. He's as mouthwatering as ever, but somehow, here in the dark, he's more tempting than ever.

"Why?" I whisper back, my heart thundering in my ears.

He leans in closer, dipping his head low enough that his lips brush the shell of my ear. "It's a surprise, *mariposita*."

"Okay, they're closed."

"Are they?" He reaches his left hand around and presses it palm down over my eyes. My pulse jumps in response to his touch. "Good. On my count. One... two... three." I feel him lean over to flip the light switch. "Now!"

I open my eyes and take in a massive red decal that matches the signage he ordered, along with the words "*it's what you do while you're alive that matters*" on the wall we painted white.

"This is too much." I try to wipe away my tears, but it is a fruitless effort, as more keep falling. "You buying the place was a godsend, but the care you're taking, the way you're truly including me and honoring my dad—Mateo, I... don't know what to say."

"Shh." He once again wraps me in his strong arms. "You don't need to say anything."

I shake my head, undoubtedly covering his shirt with my tears and snot; I am not a pretty crier. "I do, though. Honestly, there's no way I can ever repay you. You've... you're a good man, Mateo Reyes."

He releases me and steps away, shooting me a cocky grin. "The best," he challenges, all cocky-like, lightening the mood.

"Yeah, the best."

He pretends to dust his shoulder off. "I do what I can."

I don't know why, but it feels like his words have a double meaning. It's probably my emotionally over-whelmed brain reading too far into things, but it feels like more.

All of this does.

Helping me, buying the shop, the name and décor—it's too much. Far more than an acquaintance would do. More than a friend would do, even. These things, they have an intimate quality to them; one that didn't hit me until now.

Suddenly, I find myself examining every interaction we've had in a new light.

Did he ride in like a noble knight and rescue me at the fair because of his friendship with my dad, or was there something more at play?

I didn't think anything of it when I woke up in his bed —not really. But now...

My mind races faster than a Mustang at the drag strip.

His nickname, his kindness, our kiss.

Holy shit. I thought it was only a physical thing, but he actually does have feelings for me!

"What's got you looking like your brain is melting?"

I swallow roughly. *Go figure, the first guy to be interested in me for more than claiming my V-card has me so firmly in the friend zone, I may as well be a dude.*

"Just a little stunned," I answer honestly.

Mateo nods like he understands. But how could he, when we're talking about two different things. He thinks I'm referring to the shop, when really, I'm overwhelmed by him.

I want so badly to tell him how I feel—to confess that I want him, too. But he made it clear after our kiss that he had no interest in exploring anything further between us.

And I have to be okay with that. I'll show him day in and day out how much I appreciate all he's done for me. I'll be the best damn friend and employee possible... even if I break my own heart in the process.

14

MATEO

"Are you excited?" Desi asks me as she shovels cereal into her mouth.

Absentmindedly, I nod. It's our grand opening—for the mechanical side of things—and I'm still no closer to asking Seraphine to dinner tonight than I was when Mamá decreed it.

There's not really a suave way to tell a woman you're interested in but won't date that your mother is demanding to meet her.

The three stooges—Arrón, Silvi, and my traitor of a daughter—are absolutely no help either. Honestly, I think they like watching me squirm.

Desi sighs loudly, causing me to look her way. "Dad, are you listening?"

"Yes." *Mostly*, I think to myself.

"Then what did I just say?"

"You asked if I was excited."

She rolls her eyes. "No, after that."

Guilt prickles at me. "I'm sorry, *pollito*. I am lost in my mind. Say it again."

"It's okay, old man. I know your brain isn't as sharp as it once was—you know, because of your advanced age." She pauses for dramatic effect, her deep brown eyes twinkling with mischief. "I didn't actually say anything."

I groan, and she bursts out laughing.

"You think you're funny?"

"Uh, yeah. Silvi bet me twenty bucks you wouldn't fall for it, and now I'm that much richer."

"I can't believe you!" I mime plunging a knife into my heart and slump down onto the table before popping back up. "Get out of here or you'll be late for school."

She stands and moves to the sink to rinse her bowl. "Love you, Dad."

"Love you, too, Des. Don't forget about dinner tonight." She smirks. "Oh, I won't."

I don't have anyone scheduled at the shop for two more hours, but I decide to head on over. It's not like I'll do anything here other than obsess over dinner.

Unfortunately, it seems location doesn't affect my fixation; I've spent every second brainstorming ways to ask Seraphine to dinner.

As if my thoughts alone summoned her, Seraphine waltzes through the door twenty minutes early. "Good morning," she says, all sunshine and smiles as she approaches me.

She's dressed in a black logo-tee that's knotted at the

waist and a pair of skin-tight jeans that hug her lush curves. The combination is low-key and hot as hell all at once. So hot, I hardly notice the still-steaming cup of coffee she's holding out to me.

"For me?" I ask when she clears her throat.

"Yup. Drink up while it's hot."

I accept the to-go cup, deliberately making sure our fingers brush. It feels like I'm back in high school with no game. "This is twice you've brought me coffee. Don't go spoiling me."

She grins and takes a big sip of her drink. "It's nothing."

"Don't sell yourself short. You are very thoughtful." My eyes drop to her lips as she licks away a dab of whipped cream with a happy little moan.

"What can I do to help?" she asks, blessedly changing the subject, because I was two seconds away from taking her in my arms and tasting her drink straight from her lips.

"*Nada*—nothing."

"Are you sure?" Her wide eyes and pouty lips detour my thoughts back into dangerous territory. "There's not anything at all?"

Everything about her screams *fuck me*—and the worst part, I don't think she even knows it. She's an effortless blend of innocence and sin. Her dick-stirring sex appeal comes to her as naturally as breathing; it isn't something she thinks about—it just *is*.

I quickly call to mind the most unsexy thing I can think of—cutting my *abuelita's* toenails when she was sick —before answering her. "We have a few appointments on the books, and I have a few interviews, too. But for the most part, we're ready to go."

Her earlier grin returns, and since I'm apparently a schoolgirl and not a grown-ass man, I get actual butter-flies at the sight of it.

"Let's do this then!"

As she says this, Rodger and Danton—the two mechanics I hired last week—walk in.

"Morning, boys," Seraphine says with a finger wave.

Rodger grunts as he heads straight for the coffeepot. He's older than me by about twelve years and has been in the car industry for three decades. He's a little on the grumpy side, but his knowledge is priceless.

Danton, on the other hand, is only a little older than Seraphine and as green as a sapling. His eagerness more than makes up for it, though.

"Good morning, Seraphine." He practically purrs her name, and I see red; turns out his eagerness may actually get him killed.

An involuntary snarl rips from my chest, and Danton rushes to acknowledge me as well, as though his lack of a greeting was the issue. "Mateo! Glad to be here, man."

"I'll bet you are," I mutter, earning me a backhanded smack to the gut from Seraphine.

"Be nice," she scolds.

"I'm always nice."

"Be nicer, then."

"If you two are done," Rodger grouses, paper coffee cup in hand. "Maybe we can get to work?"

SERAPHINE

THE DOOR CHIMES AND I GREET THE NEWCOMER WITHOUT looking up from the computer screen. "Welcome to Dave's. I'll be right with you."

"It's you."

I lift my eyes from the screen in time to see a tall, fit guy around my age eyeing me. There's something familiar about him, but I can't quite put my finger on it.

"Um…" is all I can say, because while he seems to know me, I *think* I know him, my brain is struggling to connect the dots.

"You don't remember me?" He gives me puppy dog eyes.

I shimmy my shoulders in a shrug. "You're familiar, but I can't seem to place you."

"That's okay." He grins and I shudder. Something about him makes me feel on edge. "I'm happy to remind you. I'm Cliff."

It's obvious he's waiting for some kind of response;

only, I'm not sure what. He clearly knows me, so it's not my name he's waiting for.

"Well, it's um, nice to see you again. How can I help you today?"

His eyes light and my stomach drops. "I can think of fifty different ways, but let's start with my truck, sugar."

I blanch at the unwanted nickname. *Who does this guy think he is?* "What about it?"

"I got a new one, it needs a lift kit, wheels, tires, brush guard, the works."

"Oh." I nod my head. "We're only doing maintenance for the time being. I'm not sure when the custom side of things is set to open, but I can take your name and number?"

"Come on, sugar. Put me on the books."

"We're not accepting anyone for resto or customizations yet."

He plants his hands onto the desk and leans into my space. "Then let me take you to make up for it."

I discreetly look around the shop for Mateo or one of the guys, but there's no one. "Oh, um, I don't think…"

He reaches out, as if to touch me, and I take a small step back.

"Say *yes*, sugar. I promise we'll have a good time. And hey, you like cars… I'll let you look under my hood if you let me under yours."

Wow, that's forward. And gross. "I think I'm busy."

His eyes narrow. "I haven't said when."

Crap! I try to backpedal; he seems like the kind of guy you don't want to cross. "I just meant with the shop opening, long hours, you know… busy with work and stuff."

"Come on, now. You can't be all work and no play." He

pulls his phone from his pocket. "Let me take you to dinner tonight. You gotta eat, right?"

I shift uncomfortably on my feet. Why can't this guy take a hint?

"Tonight?" I suck in a breath through my teeth. "Tonight—"

"Tonight won't work," Mateo says, startling me. I have no clue where he came from but I am so freaking glad he's here.

Cliff's entire face hardens as he glares at Mateo with the kind of anger reserved for mortal enemies. "And why's that?"

Mateo wraps an arm around my waist and draws me into him. "Because we have dinner with my family tonight, don't we *mariposita?*"

I quickly nod my head, all too eager to play along.

"Then another night."

"No." Mateo releases me and moves me slightly behind him. "No other night. Not today, not ever. Unlike you and your friends, I know something of value when I see it and I don't share. Now, get out of here before I call the cops on you for harassing my girlfriend."

Butterflies, moths, birds, an entire menagerie of winged creatures all take flight and rip through me at his use of the G-word. I know it's only a part of his ruse, but *my God*, it feels good to hear.

"Thought she was a close family friend?"

"Guess we grew closer," Mateo deadpans.

Cliff clucks his tongue as he turns toward the door. "You're not worth the fight anyway."

"*¿Qué, pendejo?*" Mateo says, his voice a lethal mixture of disbelief and fury. "What was that?"

The unwanted patron turns back toward us, his feet rooted where he stands, as his lips tip up into a grotesque smile. "I said your *girlfriend*" —he makes sure to emphasize the word— "isn't worth the fight. I can get ass without the baggage. Ain't no pus—"

It's like a thread snaps and Mateo lunges over the counter, grabbing a fistful of Cliff's shirt and hauling him close. "You will not speak of her like that. Like she's a piece of meat. That woman is a fucking queen, and you're worth less than the gum on the bottom of someone's shoe. She is everything and you are nothing. Nothing."

"Look, I didn't mean any harm, man." Cliff's suntanned skin looks as white as a sheet as he tries to pry Mateo's hand off of him. "Just let me go, and I'll get outta here."

Mateo pulls him in closer instead. "Apologize."

"What?"

He yanks him closer still, bringing most of Cliff's body over the counter. "You heard me."

"Sorry. I'm sorry."

My knight in coveralls shoves him back, smirking as he stumbles before finding his feet. "Don't ever come back here. Your friends either."

Cliff practically runs out of the shop. As soon as the door shuts, Mateo's out from behind the counter.

"Danton!" he yells, and the younger mechanic rolls out from beneath the car he's servicing. "Come watch the front."

"Got it."

Mateo wraps an arm around my shoulders and ushers me toward the office. Before I can process it, he has us in the office with the door locked and his arms around me, holding me close.

Under different circumstances, I'd appreciate his smooth moves, but I'm currently stuck in a weird state of déjà vu.

"Why was he so familiar?"

I don't realize I'm crying until the wobbliness of my voice hits me.

Ever so softly, Mateo pulls away and wipes my tears. "You really don't know?"

I shake my head.

"Take a seat," he says, pulling out a chair and helping me into it. I expect him to grab the chair on the other side of the desk for his own use, but instead he surprises me and drops to his knees in front of me.

"He was one of the *cabrónes*—*bastards*—from the fair."

"Oh," I whisper, as memories of that night and what could have been, assault my mind. I can't help but wonder if he sought me out or if him showing up here was simply happenstance. The uncertainty has my palms sweaty and my stomach churning.

As though he can read me like a book, Mateo pulls me from the chair and onto his lap. "I will never let him hurt you, *mariposita*. I will never let anyone hurt you. Never again."

I want to wrap myself in his promises and wear them like a protective cloak. But deep down, I know they're only words. "You don't owe me anything. You don't need to pro—"

Mateo's lips land on mine, silencing me. The kiss is so unexpected, I gasp, giving him immediate entry. Our tongues swirl together in an agonizingly chaste dance before I pull away.

"What was that?" I exhale the words as I lick my own lips in an effort to savor his taste.

"You… I cannot resist you. Not always."

His confession leaves me equal parts flattered and annoyed. I decide to cut him a break and change the subject. "Seriously, though, thank you. The way you stepped in and protected me. You seem to keep saving me."

He grins. "I know a way you can make it up to me."

I climb off of his lap and stand before extending a hand down to him, as if I can actually help him up. "How's that?"

"By actually coming to a family dinner tonight."

"I'm sorry, what?"

With his eyes cast downward, Mateo scratches the back of his head. "My family is having a celebration dinner for me tonight. Please come."

"Oh." I shake my head. "I wouldn't want to intrude."

He laughs ruefully. "Would it sound crazy if I said your attendance was mandatory?"

"Says who?"

"My mother."

"Your… mother?" *Why on earth would his mother want me at a family dinner?*

"Yes. And trust me when I say, it is easier to give in to her than to fight it."

I stare at Mateo without really looking at him, lost in thought over the strangeness of the day.

"Please?" he asks, taking my hands in his.

It's that single word that seals my fate. "Sure. What time?"

16

SERAPHINE

"WHAT DOES ONE WEAR TO A FAMILY DINNER?" I ASK Magnolia, my phone pressed to my ear as I rifle through my closet.

She sighs wistfully. "I can't believe he invited you to meet his family."

"Technically, his mother did. And I already know his family—well, his siblings."

"That means she wants to meet you." Another soft sigh. "How romantic."

"I'm not so sure about that. Which is why I need to know what to wear, Mags!"

My cousin laughs. "Okay, let me switch the call to video."

Together, we narrow it down to a pair of boyfriend-cut jeans paired with a black camisole and a chunky gray cardigan.

"Wear your hair down."

"Got it. I'll call you—"

"Oh! And that necklace Myla Rose gave you last year for Christmas!"

"Okay. I'll call you—"

"And be sure to smile!"

"Magnolia! If I don't get in the shower, I won't be going at all."

"Sorry. I'm excited for you is all."

I shrug. "It's just dinner. We'll talk later tonight."

After we *finally* say our goodbyes, I fly through getting ready, opting for soft waves and a subtle makeup look.

I pass Mateo's house on the drive over and can't help but recall how waking up in his bed made me feel. Even after such a terrible night, being cocooned in his sheets and surrounded by his scent, was heaven.

His mother's house is a modest-sized craftsman style bungalow. The driveway, as well as the street in front of the house, is full with cars, so I park on the opposite side of the road.

Apprehension bubbles in my belly as I climb the steps and approach the door. My limbs feel lead-weighted and my lungs struggle to push air through. *Oh, God, why am I here?*

I should go.

I'll text Mateo and tell him something came up.

I need to go.

On shaky feet, I pivot to head back down the stairs. But the sound of the door opening has me frozen on the spot.

"*Mariposita.*" Mateo's voice wraps around me, settling my nerves in a way nothing else can. "Where are you going?"

"Oh, uh," I stammer. "To get my phone from the car. I left it."

He eyes me curiously. "Go on then. I'll wait."

Swallowing roughly, I nod before dashing across the street to my car. I pretend to look for my phone—which is nestled safely in my bag—before sliding it out and holding it up in faux-success.

I feel slightly calmer as I head back to Mateo. I wave my phone at him before slipping it back into my bag.

His eyes crinkle at the corners, like he knows I'm full of shit. Thankfully, he doesn't call me on it. "Dinner is almost ready."

"Oh, great. I'm starving," I lie, knowing full and well I probably won't be able to eat a bite.

Twining his fingers with mine, Mateo pulls me into the house after him.

"Is she here?" comes an accented yell from somewhere deeper in the home.

"*Sí, Mamá,*" Mateo replies, casting a wry grin my way.

A sudden bout of nerves sends my body to a jerking halt, as if my feet are encased in cement. The force of my stop causes Mateo to relinquish his hold on my hand, which only amplifies my anxiety.

"Seraphine," he says as he spins toward me; whatever look he sees on my face has him stepping into my space and holding me close. "Do not be nervous. My siblings already love you; Desi, too. My mother has heard so much about you, she feels like you're family already."

My breaths come in short, rapid puffs. I try to regulate my breathing, but I can't seem to drag in enough oxygen.

"Hey, hey, shh." Mateo rubs my back. "Breathe in with

me." He inhales, guiding me, and together we exhale. "Just breathe and let things happen."

The sound of muffled footsteps followed by a small gasp has us breaking apart.

"Mamá, meet Seraphine," Mateo says. "Seraphine, this is my mother, Leticia."

"*Qué bendicion*—what a blessing." His mom's voice and smile equally warm and inviting, as she approaches me with open arms.

"It's nice to meet you, Leticia," I say, holding out my hand for her to shake.

She bypasses it, going straight for a tight embrace. She smells like spices and motherly love—if such a scent exists. As she pulls away, she presses a kiss to each of my cheeks. "No, no-no. You will call me Lety."

Unexpected emotions well up within me. For this woman, who doesn't know me from a stranger off the street to be so kind and accepting, it's almost more than I can comprehend.

"Lety; okay, it's nice to meet you."

She pats my cheek tenderly and nods once. "Let us eat."

The delicious scents clinging to Lety grow stronger as she leads us through the house and into the kitchen. On the long island is a spread unlike any other I've ever seen. Platter after platter of food sits there, the wafting steam practically calling my name.

I'm so entranced by the buffet before me, I don't notice Desi approaching until she's hugging me. "Seraphine!" She rocks us back and forth. "You came! You're really here?"

I can't put my finger on it, but her words feel like they have a double meaning and I'm only privy to one of them.

"I am."

"*Menos Mal*—thank God you're here," Silvi says, bypassing me. "We can finally eat."

Even though her tone is cool, my eyes widen and my hands tremor at her words. "Am I late?" I ask, already berating myself for not getting here sooner. "Ma-Mateo said—"

Glaring at his sister, Mateo cuts me off. "You're right on time. Silvi gets hangry is all. Ignore her. Everyone else does."

Silvi sticks her tongue out at her brother. "Don't ignore me, ignore that *idiota*."

Arrón struts into the kitchen with a smile on his face. "Ignore them both," he says as he passes me a plate.

I thank him and step up to the bar, only for Mateo to take my plate. "You sit, I'll handle this."

"Are you sure?"

"Yes, go."

Lety interlocks her arm with mine and directs me to a large oak dining table. She takes the head of the table and places me to her right.

"Tell me about you," she says, her gaze never wavering.

"Um. I've lived here my entire life. I'm almost twenty-one. I like reading, cars, and makeup. Um…"

Lety waves a hand in the air. "I don't want facts and figures. I want to know *you*."

A beat of silence passes between us before I confess, "I'm not sure what that means."

"I want to know your heart. Your soul."

I have no idea how to give her what she's wanting. My confusion must be as clear as day on my face because eventually she sighs and pats my hand. "In time, then."

I'm saved from answering her by Silvi and Desi walking in. Silvi claims the chair catty-corner from me and Desi the one across from me. The food on their plates looks as good as it smells.

Arrón and Mateo follow shortly after, carrying two plates each. Arrón places one in front of Lety before rounding the table, leaving the spot beside from me open for Mateo.

He places a heaping plate down in front of me and after Lety leads us in a prayer, he begins explaining the contents of my plate to me and forking up little bites of each for me to taste.

Each bite is better than the last, and if his family finds it weird for him to feed me, no one says anything. In fact, the conversation flows so freely, I hardly give it a second thought either.

After tasting a bite of each, my favorite dish, or *guisado,* as Mateo calls it, is hands down the *tostadas de tinga.* The toasted corn tortilla—from scratch—is mindblowing on its own—seriously, I don't know how I'll ever eat a tortilla from a bag again—but when you add the refried beans and chicken, which is smoky with the exact right amount of heat, it's nearly a religious experience.

"Lety, your food, it's amazing."

She beams at my praise. "We will make you some to take home."

"If there's any left," Arrón murmurs from his end of the table, sounding full and a little sleepy.

"But first, dessert."

Desi whips around to face her grandmother. "Did you make *pastel?*"

"No, *arroz con leche.*"

"What's that?" I ask.

"A damn treat," Mateo whispers in my ear, but somehow Lety hears him and scolds him for cussing at her dinner table.

As punishment, Lety has him plate out dessert for us.

"Oh, it's like rice pudding," I say when he places a small bowl before me.

"Except better," Desi gushes, spooning up a mouthful.

I take a bite and moan happily as the flavor bursts on my tongue. I happily eat bite after bite until I'm nearly bursting at the seams, I'm so full.

Everyone is chattering quietly until Lety loudly addresses me. "Tell me, Seraphine, do you want children?"

I choke on my sip of water; add to that, it's quiet enough to hear a pin drop, and I'm thoroughly mortified.

"Ch-children?" I ask between gasping breaths.

She nods primly. "Desi needs a sibling. A boy would be nice. I've always loved the name Javier."

Mateo pushes back from the table. "*Mamá, deja de decir nombres para mi bebé inexistente.*"

"What?" I ask, utterly lost.

Desi leans over and whispers, "He told her to stop trying to name y'all's nonexistent baby."

"Ours?" I've apparently been reduced to single-word replies.

"Well, who else?" Lety asks, humor lacing her tone.

"I already told you," Mateo says. "We're not together."

Ouch, I think to myself, even though it's the truth.

His mother, though, isn't having it. "Not yet. *Terco.*" She shakes her head. "You're both stubborn."

I look around the room, hoping Desi or one of his

siblings will take our side, but none of them speak up. *Talk about an awkward end to a great evening.*

"I've already explained this to you," Mateo insists.

His mother stares him down. "And I told you to search your heart."

I scoot my chair back from the table and stand. "I think... I'm going to go. It was so nice to meet you, Lety. Thank you for a wonderful dinner." I'm already speed-walking toward the door.

"Seraphine!" Mateo yells after me.

"See you tomorrow. Thanks. Again." I swing the door open and make my escape.

17

MATEO

My mother's words after Seraphine fled last night have been on instant replay in my mind. *'You make this right, Mate!'* Like I'm the one who sent her running with talks of pregnancy and baby names.

Crazier still—my entire family sided with her. Even Desi. Aren't teen girls supposed to be stepmom averse?

They're right though—just not in the way they think. I need to make sure Seraphine understands that while my family is crazy, I am not.

The question is *how?*

Truthfully, I don't have a clue. She ignored my phone call and texts last night. But maybe breakfast this morning will soften her up toward me?

With a sort-of plan in place, I hop into my truck, grab some breakfast sandwiches, and head to the shop.

Seraphine isn't supposed to be here until eight, but I still find myself obsessively watching the clock. At five 'til, there's a knock and my heart soars, thinking it's her.

"'Morning, boss man," Danton says when I unlock the door and let him in.

I grunt in reply, retreating back behind the counter.

"Who pissed in your cornflakes?" Rodger asks, walking in behind Danton.

"Lady troubles?" the younger man asks.

Another grunt.

"That's a yes then." He pauses and sniffs the air. "Do I smell sausage?"

"Yes, but it's not for you."

Rodger and Danton exchange knowing glances, while I yet again check the clock. It's five after.

Maybe she's in traffic?

The thought's laughable. Dogwood doesn't have traffic. Not unless you end up behind a tractor.

I try to keep busy, booting up the computer and printing tickets for the day, but it's no use. My eyes keep wandering to the clock.

By fifteen after, I'm pacing the length of the shop. "Where is she?" I mumble under my breath, calling her for the second time this morning.

When I'm once again sent to voice mail, I've had enough. "Rodger!" I yell, and his head pops up from beneath the hood of the car he's working on. "Watch the shop!"

"Where ya going?" Danton asks, like it's any of his business.

"Out."

"Eyes on your own engine," Rodger commands the younger mechanic before refocusing his attention on me. "Go get her."

"Huh? Who?"

He glares. "You know who."

I don't know why, maybe because I hate the thought of being so transparent, but I play dumb and give him a puzzled look.

Like the old badass he is, Rodger calls me on my shit. "We've got this covered. Go fix whatever you messed up with *Seraphine*." He emphasizes her name.

"I... what... how?"

"You don't get to be my age without picking up a little wisdom along the way." He herds me toward the door. "Now, go fix it."

"And leave the food!" Danton calls from one of the bays.

Rodger nods his agreement.

Not wanting to waste another second, I'm out the door, in my truck, and on my way to her.

I make it to her place in record time, sighing with relief when I see her RAV4 in the driveway. At least now, I know she's here and not stranded on the side of the road somewhere.

My relief quickly gives way to frustration though. Her being here means she's intentionally avoiding me. And that won't do.

Before I can formulate a plan, I'm out of my truck, up the porch steps, and banging on her front door. "I know you're here!" I holler, a sense of déjà vu overwhelming me.

I'm prepared to hunt down the spare key—again— when the door flies open, revealing a very distressed looking Seraphine.

"Why are you here?" she asks right as I ask, "Are you okay?"

"It's not a good time."

"Let me in, *mariposita*," I say, realizing I mean it in more ways than one. I want into her home in this moment, but her heart, too.

She heaves out a longsuffering sigh and opens the door wide enough for me to enter.

I don't waste any time, hauling her straight into my arms once she closes and locks the door behind me. "Talk to me," I beg. "What's going on in that head of yours?"

She pushes against me for a brief moment before curling into me. I slide one arm behind her knees and lift her, cradling her to my chest. "Which room is yours?"

"Second door on the right," she sniffles.

I carry her down the narrow hall and into her bedroom. It's small and cheery—completely her. Seraphine clings to me as I maneuver us down onto the cramped mattress so I'm propped against the headboard and she's tucked into my side.

"Talk to me," I tell her, brushing her hair away from her face. "Tell me what is wrong."

"Everything is… just… too much."

Sensing she isn't ready to talk, I pull her closer and press a kiss to the top of her head.

After a lengthy pause, she speaks. "It's just everything, ya know? My whole life is upside down. I don't know left from right anymore. I don't even know myself anymore." Her voice cracks at the end as raw emotion pours out of her.

Gently, I tilt her face up to mine and drop a chaste kiss to her salty, tear-stained lips.

"And then there's you!"

"Me?"

"Yes! You come out of nowhere and save me over and over like I'm a damsel and you're a freaking knight."

"I wouldn't say out of nowhere. Let's be honest, we've been dancing around each other for a few years now."

"Exactly!" She shrugs out of my hold and sits up. "We went from whatever you just said, this weird holding pattern. You want me, but no—I'm forbidden! You kiss me and then say it won't happen again. Spoiler alert: it did. And then you introduce me to your family like I'm your freaking girlfriend and your mom has our nonexistent future baby's name picked out."

Her shoulders slump. "It's too much, Mateo. It's just too much."

I'm overwhelmed with this deep urge to touch her—to comfort her. Taking her hand in mine, I ask, "How can I help?"

She tugs her hand away. "I think we need boundaries."

I cock my head to the side. "How so?"

"No touching or kissing or flirting. Just friends. Nothing more."

I know I should agree to her terms and be done with it, but I... *can't.* The caveman inside of me is shouting for me to lay claim to her. Which is how I find myself countering with, "Or, you could let me take you out? On a date."

"Are you serious right now?" She shakes her head. "You're only asking me out because I told you that you couldn't."

Sitting up, I brush my knuckles over the apple of her cheek. "Don't you get it? I'm not asking you because you told me not to; I'm asking you because the thought of going without you is torture. You consume my thoughts, day and night, and I know if I don't at least try to see what this is between us, I'll never forgive myself. So, please, Seraphine. Please let me take you out?"

Her eyes fill with tears again, and I worry I've ruined us before we could even have a chance. Until she nods and whispers a teary, "Yes."

"Yes?"

"Yeah, Mateo, you can take me out."

"You won't regret it," I murmur before kissing her again.

18

SERAPHINE

"OKAY, WAIT. TELL US AGAIN," AZALEA DEMANDS AS SHE leans back into her chair at Dream Beans.

"I've told you three times!"

Myla Rose nudges me with her shoulder. "C'mon. One more time?"

I cover my face with my hands and groan. "Have you three always been so annoying?"

Magnolia laughs. "You were just as annoying when Simon was courting me."

"Oh my God!" I crack up. "You did *not* just say 'courting!'"

My cousin blushes something fierce. "Whatever. You know what I mean."

All three of my friends look back at me with wide, expectant eyes. "Fine! But I need a refill to get through this. And maybe a slice of pumpkin bread."

I push back from the table and mosey over to the counter, taking my sweet time. I even let two other patrons cut in front of me.

After I receive my order, I take the long way back to the table. I know I'm being a snot, but they are, too, so I guess we're even.

My butt isn't even in the seat before Azalea's on me. "Spill—and I mean the tea, not your coffee."

"I was upset, well, more like overwhelmed, and over-slept. I planned on calling in anyway, because the thought of facing him after his mom asked if I wanted kids was mortifying. But he showed up at the house and we talked and I told him we should just be friends."

"And then he laid one on you and asked you out?" Azalea's voice has a dream-like quality to it.

"Yup."

"So romantic," Magnolia murmurs into her mug before looking up at me. "When is y'all's date?"

"And what are you doing?" Myla Rose adds.

"Screw all of that!" Azalea slams her empty cup down onto the table. "What are you wearing?"

"This weekend and I don't know."

"Which don't you know?" my bossy blonde friend asks.

"Both. I… I've never been on a date before. Not a real one, anyway."

My confession is met with three equally stunned faces.

"I'm sorry, what?" Myla Rose asks.

I shrug. "I mean, I went to homecoming and prom, but that doesn't really count."

Azalea reaches over and squeezes my wrist. "Seraphine, are you… a virgin?"

"Um." I stare down at my lap like it holds all of the secrets of the universe.

"It's okay," Magnolia says in tandem with Azalea's, "But you're so pretty!"

"Whoa, sister-girl!" Myla Rose cries. "Giving up your V-card is a deeply personal choice and Seraphine's decision not to has nothing to do with how pretty she is."

"Thanks, Myles." I turn to Azalea. "It's not that I don't want to have sex. I just haven't."

"Well, lucky you, you'll get your cherry popped by an older, more experienced man." She wags her brows, making my cheeks flame while Myla and Magnolia giggle like schoolgirls.

"Please stop talking," I say, wishing the floor would open and swallow me whole.

"Okay, fine." Azalea stands from the table. "On one condition."

I sink lower into my chair. "What?"

"We go shopping, duh."

Mags, Myla Rose, and Azalea all offered to come over and help me get ready for my big date tonight, but I declined.

If I can't share this occasion with my father, then I don't want to share it with anyone. That may seem extreme, but he pushed me for years to date—to get out and have a life.

But how could I go out and run around without a care when he was here, dying a little more each day.

I can only imagine how tonight would go if Dad were still here.

He'd tell me the sage green playsuit Azalea picked out was too revealing and to go change. I'd roll my eyes and he'd roll his before telling me I looked beautiful.

Then he'd fuss and tell me my expertly applied

makeup was covering up my natural beauty and that I didn't need all that goop to impress a man. I'd scoff and remind him that I wore makeup for me, myself, and I.

When my date showed up, he'd definitely want to try to intimidate him—and knowing Mateo, he'd play along.

The cherry on top would be him trying to embarrass me. I can see it so clearly in my mind's eye, it's as if it's happening in real life.

I imagine he'd warn Mateo to treat me like a princess and to keep his hands and lips to himself before demanding he have me home before midnight.

But none of that is happening.

Instead, I'm getting ready with the television on for background noise.

I blink back the tears that threaten to escape. I worked too hard on my smoky eye to cry it away. But still, a tear or two escapes as I realize all of the other important firsts my dad will miss.

"Why?" I whisper out loud, even though deep down I know. I know he ended his life because he was in pain far too great to continue… and because he thought he was saving mine. And while my bitterness has lessened, my pain has not.

A knock sounds and I rush to check my eyeliner. Thank God for waterproof. I give myself one last once-over in the mirror, slide my feet into my wedged booties, and head for the door.

I open the door and am struck dumb by the sight of Mateo dressed in dark wash jeans and a form-hugging white button-down. He looks like something out of a magazine—suave and sexy and all mine, for tonight at least.

He seems to be speechless at the sight of me as well. I can only hope it's because he likes what he sees.

"*Mariposita.*" He bites down on his lower lip and looks me up and down. "*Te ves hermosa*—you look beautiful."

I duck my head as a sudden bout of nerves hits me. But Mateo's not having it. He crosses the threshold and thumbs my chin up so I'm looking him in the eyes. "Don't hide from me. Never hide from me."

"I wasn't trying to."

"Are you ready?"

"One sec." I grab my purse from the back of the sofa. "Ready."

Mateo presses a hand to the small of my back, guiding me to his GTO. Unlike my dad's classically restored one—which is under a tarp in the garage behind the house, untouched since before his death—Mateo's is modernized.

It's painted a matte gunmetal color and sits on eighteen-inch custom wheels and has been updated with power windows, racing seat belts, and a badass sound system. Whereas Dad's drove like an older car, this one drives more like a luxury car.

As he helps me into the passenger seat, I—begrudgingly—tell him it's a nice car.

Smirking, he says, "I know."

He makes sure I'm buckled before sauntering around to the driver's side. He turns the engine over and the V8 growls.

"Where are we going?" I ask.

Grinning, he ignores my question and backs out my driveway, driving us to destination unknown.

19

MATEO

From keeping my hands to myself to second-guessing my plans for the night, the drive to the destination I selected for our date is nothing short of torture.

Especially the keeping my hands to myself part.

When that door swung open, my jaw nearly hit the floor. The way her little romper-thing accentuated every curve had me vividly and eagerly imagining peeling it off.

"You're really not going to tell me?" she asks as I pull into the parking lot of our destination. "Wait—did you—is *this* where we're having our date?"

My worry over this being a mistake intensifies, but I press on.

"Trust me," is all I say as I park my car and kill the engine.

Out of my peripheral, I see her nod, and that's all the encouragement I need. "Hang tight." I exit the vehicle and sprint around to her side to help her out.

I slide the key into the main door of my garage and let

us in. As soon as she sees my setup, she gasps. "You did all of this? For me?" The tinge of wonder in her voice nearly does me in.

"Do you like it?" I ask, trying to see the space through her eyes. Are the string of lights wrapped around the car lifts too much? Is a picnic on a garage floor cheesy? Did I completely fuck this up?

"I love it," she whispers, her eyes glistening as she pops up onto her tiptoes and presses a quick kiss to my cheek. "It's amazing." She kisses my lips. "You're amazing." Her tongue darts out and licks my lips.

I oblige, letting her deepen the kiss, but only for a moment. "Slow down, *mariposita.* We have all night."

A pretty blush colors her cheeks as I lead her to the pallet of blankets I arranged on the floor. In one corner, I have a wicker basket filled to the brim with various treats as well as a cooler of water.

In another corner, I have an extra blanket and a few pillows.

But it's the back corner that holds—what I think is—the best part of all.

I guide her to a seated position in the center of the pallet. "Let me feed you." I pile a little of everything onto her plate before making one for myself. Chicken salad, toast points, an assortment of cheeses, and some fresh fruit.

The conversation flows freely as we eat; we talk about everything and nothing, and here, in my dim garage, I feel closer to this stunning woman than ever before.

Seraphine and I… we connect in a way I never thought possible; especially after losing Imani.

Yet here and now, I see every barrier that kept us apart

for what it truly was—an excuse. A way to guard my heart from what it wanted… from what it needed.

"Did you save room for dessert?" I ask as she pops her last grape into her mouth.

She pats her belly. "Dessert? I'm stuffed."

"Try a bite? Just one?" I clasp my hands under my chin in the prayer position and widen my eyes. As I knew she would, Seraphine laughs and agrees. "You won't regret it," I assure her as I retrieve the slice of chocoflan I brought for us to share.

"What is that?" she asks as I fork off a bite for her and bring it to her lips.

"*Pastel imposible*—impossible cake."

She parts her lips and I slide the tines of the fork into her mouth. She moans softly at the taste. "Oh my God. That's amazing."

"It's my dad's mom's recipe."

"Where, um, is your dad?" Seraphine asks, her eyes on her lap.

"He passed away many years ago."

"I'm sorry, Mateo."

I shake my head. "He lived a long life, a full life. He is at peace."

"You're so… wise."

"It comes with age." I wink and she giggles; the sound of it sweeter than the chocoflan.

"This night has been perfect," she says, resting her head on my shoulder.

"We're not done yet." I stand and pull her up with me. She gives me a funny look as I scoop up the bag from the back corner and pass it to her. "Put this on."

She pulls the coveralls from the bag and looks at me like I've lost it.

"You can change in the bath—"

"Turn around."

I swallow roughly and do as she says. The thought of her stripping down and changing less than two feet away has my heart pounding in my chest. The urge to turn, to sneak a peek, is strong. But I respect her and know when I see her body, it will be because she wants me to.

"Okay."

I whirl around to her and groan at the sight of her. There's nothing special about the coveralls I gave her; it's your standard run-of-the-mill coverall. Yet on her, it's pretty much porno-worthy.

She laughs like I'm joking. The tightness in the crotch of my jeans proves otherwise. But she's not ready for that —we're not ready for that.

"C'mon. We have work to do."

Her nose crinkles. "Work?"

I take her hand and guide her back into the paint booth. When she sees our project, she bursts out laughing.

"We're painting a Barbie Jeep?" I nod. "Oh my God. This is amazing."

"You're happy?"

"So, so very. What color?"

"It's for Willow."

"Pink, then."

"*Sí*."

Seraphine bounces on the balls of her feet. "I'm excited, but I gotta be honest, I've never sprayed before."

"Do not worry, *mariposita*, I will teach you." I pop the first button on my shirt. "I just need to change first."

"Do you want me to turn around?"

I shrug, and continue unbuttoning my shirt. Her pupils dilate as I shrug out of the fabric. "Do you like what you see?" I ask, knowing damn well she does.

"You're...beautiful." She slaps a hand over her mouth. "I mean handsome. Sexy. So good looking it hurts."

Stepping into her, I pull her hand away from her face and place it on my bare chest, directly over my heart. "A man can be beautiful, too. And the fact that you think I am—that you like how I look—it means something to me."

I drop my voice an octave, and drag her hand down the hard line of my abs, so it rests at the waist of my jeans. "It *does* something to me."

She sucks in a shuddery breath and dips the tip of her pinky beneath the material of my jeans. I laugh lightly and step back. "Now turn around."

"Spoilsport," she grumbles, but with a smile on her face.

"It's for me more than you," I tell her as I step out of my jeans.

"What does that even mean?"

I pull on the coveralls and step up behind her, burying my face in the crook of her neck. "I mean, seeing you react to me, to my body, makes it hard for me to resist you."

"Maybe I don't want you to resist me."

"It's only our first date."

"I'm a modern woman," she says, but her voice wobbles.

"You may be, but I'm a gentleman and want to treat you right, so that when I finally do stop resisting you, you'll be so ready for me, you'll beg."

She whimpers and squirms against me—a sure-fire sign that it's time for me to step away. "Now, let's tape this thing off, yeah?"

20

SERAPHINE

IF SOMEONE WOULD HAVE TOLD ME MY FIRST EVER DATE would take place in a garage and that I'd be painting a Powerwheel, I would have laughed.

But now that it's my reality, I couldn't imagine anything better. Who needs dinner and a movie when you could have this?

"First, we need to tape off anything we don't want painted."

Mateo demonstrates on the first faux-doorhandle before setting me free on the second.

"Now, we mix."

I rub my hands together in excitement. "I've always dreamed of painting."

Mateo wags his brows. "Then let's make your dreams come true."

He drags me over to a metal table in the corner and begins explaining the mixing process. "Since we are painting plastic, we will need to do two coats of adhesion promoter. You think you can handle that?"

"Do I do it like spray paint?"

"Yes. I would shoot it with a gun if it were a full-size vehicle, but since this is…" —he pinches his thumb and forefinger together— "*pequeño*—little, we will use this."

He passes me the can and I give it a good shake before spraying all of the exposed plastic.

I step back after the first coat, turning to him for approval. "Very good," he murmurs before starting me on the second coat.

"Now we need to lay down our base." I hang on his every word, thoroughly entranced. "Since we're doing candy, we want a metallic base—the more metallic, the better."

He mixes the base, loads the cup, and motions for me to join him. I figure he's going to have me watch, but to my surprise, he presses the paint gun into my hands and moves behind me. "We want the PSI at twenty-nine and we're going to spray from about six inches back. Smooth and fluid, yes?"

I take a deep breath, nod, and pull the trigger. The first coat goes on… well, it goes on roughly. Shooting paint from a gun is totally different than spraying with a can.

But Mateo doesn't seem too concerned. "I'll help you with the next coat."

"How long do we have to wait?"

"Fifteen minutes."

"What will we do while we wait?" I bat my lashes and bite my lip, hoping like hell I look alluring and not like a fool.

If the heated look in Mateo's eyes is anything to go by, I nailed it.

"I can think of a way or two to pass the time."

"Oh, yeah?" I ask, my voice breathy.

"Yes." He leans in and skims his lips over mine in a ghost of a kiss. "We can mix the control coat."

"You tease."

"It isn't teasing as long as you deliver, and, *mariposita,* I will deliver."

My heart flutters in my chest at the thought of him... *delivering.* "Tell me about this control coat," I say, in need of a distraction.

"We use it between the base coats and the candy to make sure there's no tiger striping."

For the next two coats of base, Mateo stands behind me, guiding my movements. His nearness makes me dizzy with need, but I shove it down, determined to impress him with my non-existent paint skills.

"For the control coat, we're going to up the PSI to thirty-one and spray the entire thing in one continuous pass. Okay?"

"Okay."

He stays behind me, our bodies perfectly aligned. I can feel the hardness of his erection pressed firmly into my backside and with every pass, I feel my panties getting wetter. *Who freaking knew painting was so sexy?*

Right when I think I can't take another second, we finish and he steps away. My body instantly misses the heat of his.

"I am going to mix the candy. Will you wipe down the Jeep with this tack tag?"

I do as he says and then we get down to work shooting the Powerwheel with four coats of candy pink and two coats of clear.

Once we finish the last coat, we stand back and admire

our handiwork. "You did good," he praises as he strips off his gloves and washes his hands.

"Thanks to my teacher."

He steps aside so I can use the sink.

"Why don't you come over here and thank me properly?" His voice is pure lust and I find myself more turned on and eager to please than ever.

I close the gap between us, skipping straight over tentative and exploring as I claim his mouth with my own. He runs his hands up and down my back, lighting me up from the inside out.

I wiggle closer to him, searching for something I can't quite name—that is, until he fists my hair with one hand and my ass with the other. I moan as he tugs my head back and slides his tongue against mine sensually.

At this point, I'm not sure who's thanking who, but as long as he never stops kissing me, I don't really care.

He shoves his knee between my legs and uses the hand on my ass to pull me flush against him. His thick erection feels like a steel rod.

Would his monster-dick even fit? I wonder as I fight the urge to rock against his thigh.

I'm so lost in him, in this kiss, that I don't realize I've lost the fight with myself until he groans and drops his other hand to my ass and begins guiding my movements.

Up, down. Up, down.

He moves my body against his in a way that sparks are flashing beneath my closed lids. My entire body trembles as euphoria like I've never felt before washes over me.

I clench my jaw to keep from crying out when the pleasure becomes unbearable. *How can he make me feel this good from just a kiss?*

"Let me hear you, *mariposita,*" he growls against my lips.

"I… I… need," I pant, unable to string enough words together to make a sentence.

"Tell me what you need and I will give it to you."

"I need…" He adds a swivel motion as he rocks me against him and my entire body convulses.

"Do you need to come, Seraphine?"

"Yes," I whine, desperate to fall into the abyss of pleasure he's holding me over.

"Can I touch you?" he asks through gritted teeth.

The fact that he's a gentleman in the heat of the moment means everything to me. "Yes, please, yes."

He tugs down the zipper of my coveralls before sliding the material from my shoulders, revealing to him my white lace bralette. "You're so fucking gorgeous." He leans down and presses a kiss to the top of each breast. "So perfect."

"Less talking," I mumble, as my eyes glaze over with want.

Mateo spins me, bringing my back to his front before snaking his hand down the opening of my coveralls. He rubs me twice over the lace of my panties before pulling them to the side and sliding his thick index finger over my slit.

"You're so wet for me, *mariposita.* So warm. I bet you taste as good as you feel."

His dirty words nearly fry my brain.

"I'm going to make you feel so good." He presses his lips to my neck, kissing and sucking at the sensitive skin as he rubs his index finger in a tight circular motion over my clit until I'm reduced to a trembling mass of embers desperate to ignite.

I open my mouth to beg for more, but as if he can anticipate my need, Mateo slides a single finger inside of me. "So tight," he rumbles, using the heel of his hand to massage my clit as he pumps in and out of me. He rocks his hips in rhythm with the white-hot pleasure he's bringing me, and something about the combined sensation of his rock-hard cock pressing into my back and the ministrations of his skilled, calloused fingers has me seeing stars.

"Oh, God. Fuck. Yes," I moan wildly, bucking my hips as my pleasure overtakes me.

I slump back against his firm body as I return to myself. My legs feel like jelly; who knew a non-self-induced orgasm could feel *that* much better.

"Are you okay?" Mateo asks, his finger still softly tracing my pussy.

"More than," I murmur, still blissed out beyond belief.

"You're beautiful when you come."

I pinch my eyes closed and don't reply, because what do you even say to that? Something tells me *thanks* is not the correct response.

He withdraws his hand from my panties and spins me to face him. My eyes widen to the size of dinner plates when he sucks his finger—the one that was *in* me—into his mouth.

"Mmm," he moans long and low, causing heat to bloom across my cheeks and down my chest. I didn't realize that was something guys actually did. I thought it only happened in books.

"Oh my God." I feel like I've been thrown into the deep end without knowing how to swim. He's so much older and more experienced than me. He's the kind of man who sucks come off of his fingers while I'm the kind of woman who's never even jacked a guy off.

Embarrassment and worry set in, robbing me of my post-orgasmic happiness. He probably thinks—

"What is wrong?" he asks, derailing my runaway thoughts.

"Nothing. It's just…" I fumble around for the zipper of my coveralls and tug it up, covering myself from his view. "I don't do things like this. Ever."

He cocks his head to the side and studies me. "When you say *things like this*, you mean what?"

"This!" I shout. "Everything that has happened tonight has been a first for me!"

I see the exact moment when the weight of my words hits him. "*¿Tú eres virgen?* You are a virgin?"

My embarrassment morphs to shame. *What would this gorgeous, experienced man want with me? I probably wouldn't even know how to please him.*

"Seraphine." He says my name so softly, almost reverently. "Answer me."

"Everything about tonight" —my voice cracks— "this was my first date. My first orgasm that wasn't at my own hands. And yes, I am a virgin."

I expect him to scoff. To laugh. To kick rocks. Instead, he scoops me up bridal-style and holds me close. "You have no idea how happy that makes me, *mariposita*."

"Ha-happy?"

He nods, brushing his nose along my temple. "That means, I'll be all of your firsts."

Holy whoa. "Those are some mighty big words for a

first date," I say, wondering if he truly means what he's saying or if it's some kind of weird bedroom talk.

"If you give me a chance, I'll show you just how much I mean them."

"This seems fast," I hedge, feeling like I'm in a dream, like I'm going to wake up alone in my bed any moment.

"This was two years coming, *mariposita.*"

"Do you mean that? Truly?"

He carries me out of the paint booth and back over to our pallet, lowering us down in the center. "*Con todo mi corazón*—with all of my heart."

I bury my face in his chest and mumble against his thundering heart, "This doesn't feel real."

"Then let me show you."

"Okay, Mateo. Show me."

21

MATEO

IN THE LIGHT OF MORNING, EVERYTHING ABOUT LAST NIGHT with Seraphine feels like a dream. From start to finish, every single detail of our date is burned into my brain like a cattle brand.

It will easily go down in the history books as one of the best nights of my life.

My phone buzzes on the nightstand. I grab it and smile when I see a text notification from Seraphine.

Seraphine: Thank you for such an amazing first date.
Me: You're very welcome. When can I see you again?
Seraphine: Uh… You'll see me Monday… at work?
Me: Ha ha. When can I take you out again?
Seraphine: OH! *face palm* I feel like an idiot.
Me: I'll make it all better on our next date.
Seraphine: You will?
Me: Always.
Seraphine: Then that's my answer, too.
Me: What is?

Seraphine: Always. Whenever you want to take me out, my answer will *always* be yes.
Me: Today?
Seraphine: Okay, I might have lied. I am babysitting Willow today.
Me: Fair enough. Desi has a basketball game on Friday. Come with me and to dinner after?
Seraphine: It's a date.

She ends her text with a winky-face emoji, which for some reason makes me smile.

I also have a text from Desi checking in. She slept over at a friend's house last night and wants to know if she can go with her friend's family to lunch and a movie today. I shoot off a reply telling her it's cool before kicking off the covers and heading to the kitchen to start a pot of coffee.

While it brews yet another text comes in.

Simon: You free today?
Me: Yeah, why? Truck's okay?
Simon: Truck is perfect.
Me: What's up?
Simon: Wanted to see if you wanted to meet up for brunch?
Me: Brunch?
Simon: Fuck off. Men can brunch, too.
Me: Sure. Why not?
Simon: Invite your brother, too, if you want.

Simon sends me the address and I forward it to Arrón, along with the time. He's smart; he'll figure out what I'm getting at.

Since I have a good three hours before… *brunch*… I decide to skip breakfast make the most of my time by mowing the lawn instead.

I throw on a pair of old jeans, a T-shirt, and boots and get to work. The entire time I work, my mind is on a certain stunning brunette and all of the firsts I promised her.

Two hours later, I'm a sweating—and slightly turned on—mess. I may have spent more time fantasizing than I did working, but the grass is cut and I have just enough time to shower before heading out.

I strip out of my grass-covered clothes and start the shower. At the first sign of steam, I pull back the curtain, step over the side of the tub, and stand under the stream of scorching water.

My mind is still on Seraphine as I lather up and scrub the sweat and grass from my skin. The memory of her soft, pleasure-filled moans fills my ears.

I squeeze my cock tightly in my fist, imagining it's her tight, virgin pussy instead. The thought of being the first —*the only*—man to touch her is almost too much.

Slowly, I jack myself, twisting my wrist on every downstroke.

In my mind, Seraphine begs. *"Harder, Mateo, fuck me harder."*

My hips buck forward as I fuck into my hand, all too willing to give in to her pleading cries.

"Fill me with your come. Oh, God, Mateo, yes!"

The idea of her begging me to come inside of her is enough to make me blow my load. I lean into the shower wall, propping myself up with one arm against the cool tile with the only thing on my mind as my release circles the drain—I can't wait until I can make that little fantasy a reality.

The place Simon told me to meet him at is a little shack of a BBQ joint in the next town over. I've never eaten at the place, much less heard of it, but judging by the jam-packed parking lot, I'm the only one.

I park my truck in the runoff lot across the street and hop out. The tantalizing smell of pecan wood and smoke practically reels me straight to the door like a fish on the line.

Inside, the mouthwatering aroma is even stronger. "Hey there, sweets, you got a reservation?"

"I'm meeting a friend."

The hostess twirls a strand of her bottle-blonde hair around her finger. "Is she here already?"

"He," I correct, scanning the small space for Simon. "And yeah, I see him."

I slide past her without another word, and head for Simon. Cash, Drake, and my brother are here with him.

"Mateo." Simon stands as I approach. "Glad you could make it, man." We do the back-slap-man-hug thing.

The other guys quickly greet me and our server swings by and grabs my drink order.

"Y'all come here often?" I ask, reading over the paper menu.

"Once a month," Drake tells me. "Try the brisket."

Cash shakes his head. "Man, fuck the brisket. Get the pork."

"You're both wrong," Simon says. "The burnt ends are where it's at."

I exchange a glance with my brother, knowing we're both going to get the potato cakes with runny eggs and burnt ends.

Once our orders are placed, my brother knocks his knee into mine under the table. "How'd last night go?"

All three of the other men turn to look at me. "Big plans last night?" Simon asks.

"He had a date," Arrón tells them. "With Seraphine."

"Not exactly what I had in mind when I asked you to check on her."

Shit. My heart thunders in my chest. "It, uh… it just happened, you know?" The thought of losing him as a friend sucks, but Seraphine's worth any bridge I might burn. "I'm sorry I didn't tell you."

"Like I didn't already know." He narrows his eyes and glares at me before grinning. "But I'm glad it's you. Magnolia thinks you're good for her. And if my Goldilocks approves, I do, too."

"That means a lot to me."

"But if you hurt her, I'll kill you." He jabs his plastic spork my way as he speaks. It's probably not as threatening as a knife would be, but he gets his point across.

"Back to last night though," my brother urges. He's probably dying to know since I recruited him to help me set everything up at the shop.

"It was… perfect. Better than perfect…" My words fall away as doubt presses against my newfound contentedness.

"I feel like there's a *but*," Cash says.

"I mean, shit." It is a struggle to compose my thoughts

into intelligible words. "I didn't plan on her, you know? She kind of blindsided me. I've only taken her on one date and—" My words die in my throat.

"What?" my brother asks. "What is it?"

"Dios mio carajo creo que la amo."

Simon and Arrón both suck in harsh breaths.

"Well, *Jefecita* called that one." My brother smirks as he leans back in his chair, without a single care in the world.

"Translation please?" Drake asks, his eyes wide in confusion.

When I don't reply, Arrón does for me. "Dipshit just realized he's in love."

Denial sets in and I shake my head. "No. That's crazy, right? We've been on one date." Even as I say the words, I know my truth. I love Seraphine Reynolds.

"I don't know, man." Cash shrugs. "I pretty much fell for Myla Rose on the spot."

Drake laughs. "My Azalea addiction pretty much started before puberty."

I turn to Simon and he nods. "When you know… you know."

22

SERAPHINE

Mateo and I texted on and off all weekend. We played our own little version of Twenty Questions. It involved some semi-scandalous pics—and, well, my phone definitely has a new home screen.

One I found myself shamelessly staring at many times over the last two days.

But now, it's Monday morning and I'll be seeing him in person for the first time since our date.

Nerves flutter all throughout me, battering my insides like birds trying to fly while caged. Is he going to be the same Mateo he was before our date, or will he be the affectionate and touchy man from our date? Or worse yet, will he become the picture of professionalism and treat me like his employee?

I guess I'm fine with any of the above; it's more so the not-knowing that has me fretting.

Which is why I'm wearing my best armor—makeup. The look is subtle, almost natural-looking, but it is high-lighted and contoured to perfection. My brows are sculpted, my liner winged, my lashes full, and my lips glossy.

It also happens to be the exact way I wore my makeup on our date. So, even if nothing comes of my little power play, Mateo's reaction will be worth how early I woke up to look like this.

I waltz into the shop at a quarter to eight, a tray of coffees in hand. "Morning!" I holler in the empty garage. "I brought caffeinated beverages!"

"Regular coffee or that fancy shit?" Rodger asks, coming from somewhere past the first bay.

I grin. "Regular for you."

"Good."

I hear the door to the back office open and close. Looking up, I see Danton heading my way with Mateo hot on his heels.

Danton whistles when he sees me, but Mateo doesn't look impressed. My gut clenches as I worry this was a mistake.

"My office," Mateo growls before pivoting around and stomping back the way he came.

"I got you a mocha," I whisper to Danton, passing him the tray, leaving both mine and Mateo's drinks behind.

I walk toward the office like I'm heading to my execution—slowly and with great trepidation.

As I approach the door, Mateo swings it open, grabs my wrist, and yanks me inside. I'm ready for him to yell, expecting it even. So, when he leans down and kisses me like his life depends on it, I'm caught off guard.

He slides his tongue past my lips and tangles it with my own in a passionate but unexpected kiss.

When the need to breathe becomes too great, we both break away panting.

"What was that?" I ask, my chest heaving.

"You look... I could not resist you." He dips back down and captures my lips once again.

He kisses his way from my lips to my jaw and down my neck. I rise on to my tiptoes, angling my face just so to give him better access—something he readily takes as he sucks and licks and nips at the sensitive skin at the crook of my neck.

A moan slips past my lips as I thread my fingers into his hair, tugging to bring his mouth back to mine.

He palms my ass and squeezes gently before pulling away, placing one last soft kiss on my lips.

"So, you're not mad?"

"Mad? No. Turned on beyond belief? Hell yes."

"I brought coffee..." I offer lamely.

Mateo's eyes crinkle at the corners as he smiles. "A kiss from you wakes me up better than coffee ever could."

"Flattery will get you everywhere."

"You deserve more than empty words, Seraphine, and I plan to only ever speak truth to you. So, when I tell you something, know that I mean it."

"How do you always know the right thing to say?"

He taps his temple. "Age... wisdom... remember?"

I roll my eyes and laugh under my breath. "The other day, I suggested ground rules. Maybe we should revisit?"

"My instinct is to tell you no, so why don't you tell me why?"

I was hoping he'd agree with me right off the bat. "Um, I don't know. I just think... maybe some guidelines for when we're at work?"

"Guidelines like what? Like no kissing you or touching you?"

"Yeah, things like that."

He looks down at his feet and shakes his head before lifting his gaze to mine. "No."

"No?"

"Life is too short, *mariposita*. While I will always respect you, I will not hide how I feel for you. I've spent two years denying myself—no more."

I feel like the little animated guy from the Red Bull commercials; only instead of an energy drink, it's Mateo that is giving me wings.

Like a lovesick lunatic, I launch myself at him. He expertly catches me, guiding my legs around his waist and spinning us so my ass is propped on the ledge of his desk.

"You're so damn gorgeous," he murmurs, leaning in. His lips are a hairsbreadth away when a jarring knock on the office door breaks us apart.

"What?" Mateo barks, one hand still on my ass and the other still tangled in my hair.

"The, uh, new hire is here," Danton says from the other side of the door.

Mateo swears under his breath. "Tell him I'll be right with him."

I glance down at the space where our bodies are aligned. Mateo's desire for me is very prominent; I can't help but grin at his predicament.

"Here's your first job as shop manager." He steps back and helps me to my feet. "Give the new guy his paperwork while I calm down." He kisses me softly. "Think you can handle that?"

"I'd rather handle you," I singsong as I skip to the door.

He groans as I open the door and slip over the threshold and back onto the garage floor.

I stop by the restroom and fix my smeared makeup and tousled hair as best as I can before hurrying to the front to meet our new hire.

"'Bout time," Rodger grouses under his breath as I approach.

Ignoring the grumpy older mechanic, I paste on my customer service smile and address the newcomer. "Hi, you must be Ryker."

The man before practically oozes bad-boy pheromones and judging from the cocky smirk on his lips, he knows it.

"And you are?"

My cheeks heat. My back office make-out sesh with Mateo has me more than a little flustered. "Sorry. I'm Seraphine."

"What's your role here?" he asks, looking from me to Danton and Rodger.

"I'm the manager."

Ryker's lips twitch like he wants to laugh.

"Something funny?" I cross my arms over my chest and glower.

"Just wondering what your qualifications are, is all."

Why did Mateo hire this jackass? And why did he not tell me he was such *a jackass?*

Danton and Rodger exchange worried looks.

"I don't see how my qualifications affect your ability to do your job."

He tips his head back a fraction of an inch and breathes out a laugh. "Got it."

"I don't think you do. This shop was my father's.

Mateo owns it now, but it's my dad's name on the sign. I grew up here. I may have a vagina, but I assure you it doesn't hamper my ability to do my job and it damn sure shouldn't affect your ability to do yours."

"Breathe, *mariposita*," Mateo says, startling me. I'm not sure how much of that he heard, but I stand by everything I said.

Ryker eyes Mateo's nearness to me and grins like suddenly my presence here makes sense.

"Everything okay here?" Mateo asks no one in particular.

We all remain silent until Danton says, "Yup, your girl was just setting the new hire straight."

"Straight about what?" Mateo's voice is low with menace.

"About whether or not I'm suited to my position here."

Mateo rubs a hand over his chin before turning to Ryker. "Why don't we go have a talk?"

Ryker's eyes dart between me and the guys before he nods and follows Mateo back to the office.

As soon as they're out of sight, Danton cracks up. "Let's hope he doesn't give new guy the same kind of talk he gave you."

"Men in this industry can be real assholes," I grumble.

"We are." Rodger nods solemnly, but there's a twinkle in his eye. "Now, get to work. We've all fucked around enough this morning." He gives me a pointed look. "Some of us more than others."

MATEO

THIS ENTIRE WEEK HAS BEEN A LESSON IN PATIENCE—BUT it's finally Friday.

"You ready to head out?" I ask Seraphine, diverting her concentration from whatever she's showing Ryker on the computer to me.

After my talk with him Monday, he's been a model of respect toward Seraphine.

Gracias a Dio—thank God—because I would've hated to fire him with the credentials he's packing. But for her? I'd do it in a heartbeat.

"Almost done." She smiles sweetly before turning back to her task. "You can head out; I'll meet you there."

My lip curls at the idea. "Or we could go now?"

She laughs. "Go home, caveman. I need to freshen up before the game anyway."

Wisely, Ryker keeps his eyes on the computer screen. "Fine," I concede, "but I'm picking you up."

Seraphine bites down on her bottom lip, trapping the smile I see trying to break free. "Sounds good."

"I'll be there at six."

I stalk back around the counter and press a lingering kiss to her lips.

Ryker clears his throat. "Sooner we finish, sooner you can get out of here."

With reluctance, I pull away and give her a meaningful look. "Then get back to work." I pause at the door. "Oh, and, Seraphine, pack a bag."

I pull into Seraphine's driveway with five minutes to spare. Much to my surprise, she's out on the porch with a small overnight bag resting at her feet waiting on me.

As soon as I shift the truck into park, she's bounding down the stairs and climbing up into the cab beside me.

"Miss me?" I look at her over the top of my sunglasses.

"Depends." She taps her lip, pretending to think. "How lame would it be for me to say yes when I saw you less than an hour ago?"

I laugh as I throw the truck back into gear. "Then we can be lame together."

She reaches over and places her hand over mine on the shifter, rubbing her fingers over my knuckles. "Together...I like the sound of that."

"I can't help but notice you packed a bag."

A soft, melodious laughs bubbles out of her. "Well, this very bossy man told me to."

"Mmm, really?"

"Yeah and as it turns out, I kind of like it when he orders me around."

I damn near swerve off the road as images of all the other ways she might like me bossing her around.

"Are you nervous?" I flip my hand and interlace our fingers. Her inexperience would bother a lot of men, but to me, it means I'll be the one to teach her—and even if it doesn't happen tonight, I know I'll be the one to have the honor of helping her learn what she likes.

"Maybe. But only a little."

"Nothing has to happen between us, I just want to wake up next to you."

Seraphine falls quiet, her fingers tensing against mine. I worry I came on too strong, until she says, "Or...something...could happen."

Fuck. Me.

My cock twitches in my pants. She's this beguiling mixture of shy and bold, and truth be told, the combination really works for me.

"Sure." I bring her hand up to my lips and kiss her knuckles. "But only what you want to happen. There's no rush." The words are a little painful to say, because Lord knows, the thought of sliding into her sweet pussy is enough to drive me mad, but I respect her more than enough to wait until she's ready.

"There is if we don't want to be late for the game!"

It takes me a second to process the subject change. "We're going to make it."

"Told you," I tell her, five minutes later, when we're parked, out of the truck, and in line to get tickets.

"Only because you drove like a madman."

"How many?" the PTA mom at the door asks.

"Two please." After paying, Seraphine and I head into

the crowded gymnasium hand-in-hand. Luck's on our side and we find an open spot on the second row of the bleachers, mid-court.

"How long has Des been playing basketball?"

My heart swells at the sound of Seraphine calling her *Des*. "Since she was old enough for city league. But this is her first varsity game."

"That's exciting. I don't think there's anything I've liked that long."

"Cars," I tell her, bumping my shoulder into hers.

"That's true. Does she want to play in college?"

"Depends on the day you ask her, but most likely, yes."

Before Seraphine can respond, the lights flicker and a pounding bassline fills the gym. "Ladies and gentlemen," the announcer booms, "let's give it up for the four-time state champs, the Lady Dolphins!"

Strobe lights flash and everyone on our side of the bleachers goes wild, Seraphine included.

From there, the starting players are called out, including my girl. "Number fourteen, point guard, Desi Reyes!" I whoop and cheer so loud for my girl I miss most of her stats; good thing I know them by heart.

The game starts fast and moves even faster. The girls on the court are all here to win. Seraphine claps and cheers with me as Desi runs up and down the court, holding her own during her varsity debut.

By the fourth quarter, the game is tied and everyone—players and spectators alike—are tense. There are only seconds on the clock when Desi manages to steal the ball. With lightning-quick speed and damn near robotic precision, she maneuvers back down the court before.

"Shoot!" her coach yells as the clock rapidly counts down.

She stops at the three-point line and launches the ball like it's a grenade and the goal's her target. I hold my breath, feeling frozen in place, until the ball sails through the hoop, nothing but net.

The buzzer sounds.

The crowd goes wild.

My girl just scored the winning point in her first varsity game.

"Mateo," Seraphine yells over the cacophony of sound, "she's amazing!"

"C'mon, let's go talk to her before she heads into the locker room."

"Did you see me?" Desi yells, still hyped from the game.

"You were—"

My daughter bypasses me and damn near tackles Seraphine with a sweaty bear hug. "Did you see me?" she asks again.

"I did!" Seraphine rocks and jumps, holding Desi close. "You're a freaking beast!"

They whisper to one another for a minute before breaking apart. Desi flings herself at me and, even though I was her second choice, I can't be mad. The fact that she even likes Seraphine blows my mind. "You did so good, pollito. I am so proud of you."

She beams. "Thanks!"

"Be safe tonight. No parties. No boys. No drinking."

My daughter sighs. "How about yes to a party—with the team—and no to boys and booze?"

"Deal. Check in regularly."

"I will, Dad." Her eyes flit between Seraphine and me. "Y'all have a good night and, uh, be safe, too." She winks and dashes away before I can fully register what she said.

SERAPHINE

"I still can't believe she hugged you first—my own flesh and blood," Mateo says as we walk into Trattoria, Dogwood's go-to Italian restaurant.

"Forget that." My cheeks heat before I give voice to my thoughts. "I'm still dying over her telling us to *be safe*."

Mateo yanks his hand from mine and covers his ears. "La-la-la—I don't want to hear that shit!"

I tug on his elbow and pull his hands away. "She's sixteen, Mateo."

He nods. "Only two more years until I can send her off to a monastery."

It's a struggle not to cackle as we approach the hostess stand, but through Herculean effort, I manage it.

We're shown to an intimate booth near the back of the dining room. The low lighting and soft music make for a romantic setting, but I'd be happy just about anywhere with this man.

The strength of my feelings for him is honestly a little scary. My once unrequited—or so I thought—crush has morphed into this larger-than-life thing. Mateo's my friend, my protector, and if I have any say in the matter, after tonight, he'll also become my lover.

"Have you eaten here before?" he asks after we place our drink orders—a beer for him and a Coke for me.

"Once."

"Do you know what you're getting?"

"Not a clue; everything sounds good," I groan. "What about you?"

"The sweet potato ravioli. It's out of this world."

I hum under my breath and read the menu over again. Everything sounds delicious, but my mind keeps straying away from my choices and back to the game.

Mateo's the kind of dad every daughter deserves—the kind I had. Desi is his entire world and seeing him cheer and clap and scream for her at her game only made my feelings for him that much stronger. The pride on his face as she shot the winning goal may have been directed at her, but it was a bullseye to my heartstrings.

I finally focus and manage to narrow it down to two options by the time our server arrives, but they both sound delicious. I gesture for Mateo to order first, but I'm still no closer to choosing when he's done.

"Do you trust me, *mariposita*?"

He's asked me this before, but tonight, it seems to carry more weight. He's shown me over and over that he's worthy of not only my trust, but my love, too. But that's a whole other issue that I'm not getting into tonight.

"You know I do," I murmur, sliding my calf against his under the table.

"Enough to order for you?" He reaches beneath the table and pulls my foot into his lap. With a touch lighter than that of a feather, he skims his fingertips up and down my leg.

Shivering, I nod.

"My beautiful date will have the Tuscan roast chicken with the ricotta gnocchi."

Over the course of our meal—our insanely delicious meal—we talk about everything under the sun. From our childhood memories to cars to Desi's mood swings. The conversation between us flows like a river; I can't imagine us ever running out of things to talk about.

But more than that, it is the little touches that really do me in. A graze of my hand, or a brush of his leg. He has my skin tingling in anticipation and my panties wet, all without even trying.

"Would y'all like dessert?" our server asks, snapping me out my lustful thoughts.

I shake my head no. I'm ready to get him home so we can—*hopefully*—whip up our own after dinner treat. God knows, he probably tastes better than anything on the menu—which is saying a lot because the food here is delicious.

"Yes, please," Mateo tells her and I deflate a little.

Maybe we're not on the same page after all. Did my inexperience mislead me? Does he really only want to wake up next to me?

"A slice of the limoncello cheesecake—to go." He winks at me and my heart soars into my chest as hope fills me.

I know I should be more nervous than I am about potentially punching my V-card; I am, but I'm excited, too. I couldn't think of a better person to give it up to. Mateo's worthy of my cherry; he's kind, thoughtful, respectful, and most of all, he's shown me over and over that he values me. He wants more than my body; he also appreciates my mind.

Once our bill is paid, Mateo scoops up our to-go box with one hand and extends the other to me, helping me from my chair. He presses a quick kiss to my lips and wraps an arm around me, holding me close as we walk back to his truck.

"Thank you for dinner," I murmur as he helps me into the passenger seat. As he walks around to the driver's side, I can't help but wonder whether he has the same thing in mind for when we get back to his place.

"Of course, *mariposita*, it was my pleasure."

The way his tongue wraps around the word *pleasure* turns my skin to gooseflesh. Anticipation thrums through me, mingling with my desire.

I have to squeeze my thighs together to try and alleviate the ache pulsing between them.

"Are you okay?" Mateo asks, mistaking my arousal for discomfort.

"I will be," I whisper into the darkened cab of the truck.

"You will be?" His tone is riddled with confusion at my cryptic words.

Nodding, I reach over and place my hand on his thigh, rubbing my thumb over the inside seam of his jeans, only centimeters from his dick.

He groans and shifts in his seat. "You keep that up and we're going to have a problem."

"Then take me home," I beg him, "and I'll show you what a good problem solver I am."

25

MATEO

"You can't say things like that," I groan at the little vixen next to me. She has my dick hard enough to pound nails and my right foot pressing the accelerator into the floorboard.

"Say what?" she asks, all innocent like.

She *is* innocent, but I can sense the dirty girl inside of her begging to break free.

"These innuendos…they're enough to make me wreck this truck."

Seraphine hums under her breath as she rubs her pinky finger over my dick. Even through my jeans, the sensation of her touch makes my entire body shudder.

I sigh in relief when my street comes into view; I've never been so anxious to get home in my entire life.

"We wouldn't want that," comes her soft reply. She withdraws her hand from my lap. My eyes flash to her and she smirks. "Gotta make sure we make it home safe so we can have our dessert."

"You mean the cheesecake?" I croak, desperate for

clarification. Truthfully, even if all we do is kiss, I'm so damn hot for her, I'll gladly lap up anything she gives me.

"No," she whispers, "I mean you…and me…"

My grip on the steering wheel is white knuckled. "You and me what?"

She sucks in a deep breath. "On our last date, you ta-tasted me and I…well…I want to taste you, too."

Fuuuuuck.

I hit the gas when my driveway comes into view; my tires squeal as I whip into the garage, killing the engine before I'm fully out of gear. "Stay put," I order, practically flying out of the truck and running to her side.

Seraphine giggles at my antics but I don't care. She can laugh all she wants, as long as I get to feel her pouty lips wrapped around my dick.

I scoop her into my arms and toss her over my shoulder, carrying her into the house.

"Put me down, you brute." She laughs as I stalk through the dark house toward my bedroom.

I set her down onto the bed and flip on the lamp on my nightstand. We stare at each other for a moment; she looks more stunning than ever in the soft glow of the light.

"Take your shirt off," she whispers, bolder than I ever imagined she'd be.

"Only if you do, too."

With zero hesitation, she whips her shirt off and throws it at my feet.

I take it a step farther and shed my jeans as well, leaving me in nothing but my boxers.

Seraphine eats me up with her eyes. "Can I touch you?"

I think I'm heaven.

"God, yes, please."

She crawls across the mattress to where I'm standing at the side of the bed. Her pupils are dilated and her breaths shallow as she reaches her right hand up and trails her fingers up and over the dips and valleys of my abs, all the way to my pecs.

I hiss out a breath as she drags her thumb over one of my nipples.

"Do you like that?" she asks in earnest.

"*Mariposita*, I'd like just about anything you want to do to me."

She nods to my tented boxers. "Can I touch you there?"

"Anywhere. You can touch me anywhere."

She moves her hand back down my body with a deliberate slowness that sets every nerve ending on fire. I expect her to cup me over my boxers, but she skips the pre-game and goes straight for the main event, slipping her hand beneath the elastic band.

Seraphine has me so keyed up, the simple friction of her palm sliding over my rigid cock has me ready to explode.

Now it's my breaths that are coming shallow. Maintaining my composure while she leisurely explores my body is quite possibly the hardest thing I've ever done.

Especially when she tugs down my boxers, exposing me fully.

"Jesus Christ, Mateo." She pumps her hand over the length, squeezing me at the base. "There's no way—it won't fit."

I thread my fingers through her hair, tugging on the

long strands to lift her face to mine. The sight of her, topless on my bed, is something I'll remember for the rest of my days. She has the face of an angel and a body made for sin.

"It will, *mariposita*. I promise you."

She licks her lips before lowering her back down to where she's still working me over. Time stops as she leans forward and presses a kiss to the head of my dick before sucking it into her mouth.

"*Lo haces tan bien,*" I grunt as my hips buck forward.

She pulls back with an audible pop. "Did you not like that?"

The worry in her tone dispels my lust enough to bring me back down to earth.

"Liked it too much—you're very, *very* good at that."

"Oh." She chuckles and draws me into her mouth again.

Her head bobs up and down as she sucks me. While her movements are sloppy and her technique unrefined, I meant what I said. Plus, knowing the honor of her first blow job is being bestowed upon me more than makes up for it.

I cup her cheek and she pulls away again. "Tell me what you like."

Yup, definitely in heaven.

"Wrap your hand around the base and your lips around the tip. Work them together, in time with each other."

She does as I say, sucking and jerking me in tandem.

"A little harder." She listens beautifully. "God, yes." I tip my head back and groan.

A tell-tale tingle starts in the base of my spine and my hips buck forward on their own accord.

"Your mouth feels too good, *mariposita.*" I thread my fingers through her hair and gently guide her movements.

Her answering moan has my back arching and my jaw clenching. "I'm close. Fuck. Play with my—" I draw up short when I glance down and see the hand not wrapped around my dick shoved between her legs, her hips rocking.

That right there is what does me in. "Gonna come," I tell her with barely enough time to pull my pulsing cock from her hot, wet mouth.

I finish long and hard, all over her chest. The sight of the milky ropes against her tan skin is a sight to behold. "Fuck, Seraphine."

She runs a finger through my release and looks up at me. "You liked it?"

"I loved it."

Nodding, she brings her finger to her mouth and sucks my come from it. My knees go weak and my heart thunders in my chest. Her nose scrunches at the taste, but she swallows it down with a pleased smile.

How can she be so fucking adorable and sexy all at once?

"Good. I...I think I did, too."

"Yeah?"

She nods.

"Got something else you might like better."

"What?" She bites her lower lip.

"Hang tight." I run to the bathroom, wet a washcloth, and return to her. I wipe the rest of my release from her chest—even if seeing it there lights something primal inside of me on fire.

I trace the lace edge of her bra. "Can I take this off?"

"Yes. Please."

With deft fingers, I reach around and unhook her bra. The straps slide partway down her shoulders, but Seraphine pulls it the rest of the way off. Her breasts are perky and full, perfect tear drops, topped with taut dusky nipples just begging for my mouth.

Licking my lips, I lean in and lay my lips against hers. "You're a goddess."

Seraphine hums and draws my lower lip into her mouth, sucking lightly before deepening our kiss.

I drag the back of my fingers up her sides, following her curves around to cup her breasts. I test their weight as I kiss my way down her neck.

She releases a shaky breath as I move even lower, sucking one pebbled nipple into my mouth. I kiss and suck and nibble until she's panting before moving to the next.

I feel her fingers push through my hair before digging into my scalp. For a split second, I worry she's going to push me away, but she doesn't. No, she pulls me closer, moaning in pleasure at my ministrations.

"Does that feel good?"

"Yes!" She arches into me.

"There's somewhere I can kiss you that'll feel even better."

"Where?" she asks, causing me to chuckle. "Oh!" She pushes my head back. "Are...are you sure?"

"Only if you are," I answer honestly.

"I...I...um." She flexes her fingers in her lap before reaching up and popping the button on her jeans. "I want to at least try it."

"If you want me to stop, all you gotta do is say so and I will."

"Really?"

"Really."

She rises to her knees and I help her slide her jeans and panties down as far as we can. I help her to lie back before removing the offending garments the rest of the way.

I part her thighs and crawl between, peppering alternating kisses as I go. She covers herself with both hands before I can reach the promised land.

"Are you scared?"

"A little."

I kiss her fingers. "Do you want me to stop?"

"No." She removes one hand and lays it at her side. "Keep going." And then the other.

"Tell me if it's too much," I murmur, before placing a hot, open mouthed kiss to her pussy. "*Me encanta como sabes*—I love how you taste."

Seraphine fists the sheets, shifting her hips.

I reach up and splay my hand across her belly, effectively holding her still.

"Let me make you feel good." I lick her from the bottom of her slit, darting my tongue inside, before flicking her clit with the tip of my tongue.

"Oh," she whimpers, "my God."

"That's right, *mariposita*, enjoy the way I make you feel." I lick and suck and fuck her with my tongue until any and every hint of her former nervousness is gone and she's bucking against my face.

"Shit, Mateo-ohhh." She draws out the 'O' as she drives her fingers into my hair. The sting at my scalp is the feeling of a job well done, but I won't stop until she's screaming my name. "I...need...I—"

"Shh." I blow on her clit. "I've got you; I know what you need."

I slide the hand from her belly down between her legs, dragging my index finger between her swollen, wet lips before ever-so-gently slipping it inside of her. I curl it, rubbing against her sweet spot a few times before adding a second finger.

She winces a little as I stretch her, but I lean back down and lick the ache away. My mouth and fingers work together to bring her nothing but pleasure.

Her pussy clenches around my fingers and I latch onto her clit, sucking hard until her entire body tenses and she screams my name.

I press gentle kisses all over her thighs and belly until her body comes down from its high. "That was...wow."

26

SERAPHINE

Mateo looks up at me with an almost loving look in his brown eyes. "Let me clean you up."

He reaches for the wash rag on his nightstand, but I grab his wrist. "Wait."

"What's wrong?" he asks, his brow raised in alarm at my pleading tone.

It takes me a second to work up the courage. *You can do this! You know he cares for you. The worst he can say is no. But please, God, don't let him say no!*

"I...I want you to, um." I stop and inhale deeply before continuing. "I want you to f-fuck me."

I nod, pleased with myself for only sounding a little foolish.

Mateo looks down at me. His lips are in a firm line, but his eyes are shining. "Are you sure?"

"Yes." I twine my arms around his neck and pull him down onto me. "Please. I...I want to give myself to you completely."

Another low groan rips through him. "I cannot tell you no."

"Good." I slide my lips over his, surprised by the way I taste on his lips. "I don't want you to."

"It's going to hurt." He reaches down between us and rubs his index and middle fingers over my still sensitive flesh.

I spread my knees wider. "I know."

"I don't want to hurt you."

"It's worth it." I kiss him again and shift my hips toward him. "Plus, you can make it up to me next time."

He spreads me with his fingers, and little by little, he begins to work himself in.

My body tenses at the first tinge of pain and Mateo immediately stops. "Do you want me to keep going?"

Tears dot my lashes, but I nod.

"Are you sure? We can stop."

"No, please. Keep going."

He lowers his lips to mine and kisses me. "I'm so sorry, *mariposita*."

He pushes forward again and it feels like I'm being split in two. I whimper as he pushes through and seats himself full inside of me. "Oh. Oh, God."

Mateo moves from my lips and kisses away the tears trailing my cheeks. His face is pinched in concentration and his body stock still.

"It's okay, I'm okay."

"I hate that I'm hurting you."

"It won't always feel like this, right?"

"No. It won't."

I nod, sniffling. "Okay then."

As gently as possible, he shifts up onto his knees. Even

in pain, I take the time to appreciate the work of art that is his body. He's all fine lines, lean muscle, tanned skin, and ink.

"Let me try," he mumbles to himself before pressing his thumb to my clit. He rubs me in tight circles until the screaming pain softens to a dull roar. "You're so beautiful. *Te sientes tan bien*—you feel so good. I..."

"You can move," I wheeze, my body caught in an inky abyss of pain and pleasure. "I'm...I'll be okay."

He pulls his hips back a fraction before shifting them forward. His thrusts are slow, gentle, deliberate. He's more worried about my discomfort than he is his orgasm. That alone tells me that giving him my V-card was the right decision.

"*Podría quedarme dentro de tipara siempre.*" Mateo brushes my hair from my face. "I could stay inside you forever."

The emotion behind his words sends my heart tumbling down into my belly.

Even as sweat beads his brow, his thrusts remain slow and steady. Little zips of pleasure spark through me as he rubs my clit.

"Fuck," he grunts. "I wanted to make you come, but I'm not going to last."

Mateo's rhythm falters as he swells within me. I sigh as his release fills me.

Oh. God. Oh, no.

He murmurs sweet nothings into my ear as he pulls out of me, but my mind is suddenly a million miles away.

"Are you okay?" he asks, worry etched into his every feature. "Did I hurt you?"

"We...um...a condom."

His brow furrows as realization dawns. "Fuck. Seraphine. I—I'm so sorry. I should have made sure." He stands and paces alongside the bed. "You entrusted me with something so precious and I didn't even think to protect you!"

"Mateo." His name leaves my lips on a soft cry.

In a flash, he's back on the bed, hefting me onto his lap. "Are you on birth control?"

I shake my head as panic dots my vision. *He's going to hate me...he's going to be so mad. I bet he regrets ever—*

"Get out of your head, *mariposita.* If anyone here is to blame, it is me. I failed you and I am sorry."

"It's not your fault; it's *our* fault."

Mateo holds me against his chest and strokes my hair. "It'll be okay."

I sniffle. "What if—"

He tilts my head up and captures my lips in a kiss so tender it makes my insides feel like jelly. "Come what may, Seraphine, we will be fine."

"Are...are you sure?" I ask, because how could he possibly mean that?

"*Eres mi vida,*" he whispers so quietly I'm not sure if he even really spoke at all.

"What?"

"*Nada*—it is nothing for you to worry about." He moves me from his lap to the mattress and stands. "Let's get you cleaned up."

He takes my hand in his and ushers me into the bathroom. I'm grateful for his guidance, because my mind is currently like the ball in a pinball machine—it's rocketing around, bouncing violently off every *what-if* imaginable.

He releases my hand and kneels in front of the tub. I

tie my hair up into a bun as he starts a bath, adding a healthy squeeze of his own bodywash for bubbles. "In you go," he quietly orders.

The warm water soothes my skin and the scent of his soap tickles my nose and calms the ricocheting thoughts of my brain.

"Can I wash you?"

His question surprises me, but I guess it shouldn't; Mateo is a gentleman through and through.

"Sure."

He grabs another washcloth and wets it before squirting a dollop of his bodywash onto it. With a softness that belies his size, he washes me from head to toe, taking special care between my legs.

"Are you sore?" he asks when I wince.

"Only a little."

He looks troubled at the thought of me being in pain— even if it is minimal and oh-so-worth it. "Hey, it's okay. I don't have any regrets."

As soon as the words leave my lips, the truth of them settles over me. Even though we didn't use protection, I have no regrets. Sure, it was a reckless mistake and could have some pretty intense consequences, but Mateo said we would be okay no matter what, and maybe it makes me foolish, but I believe him.

"Tonight, what you gave me," he says, "was a gift. Thank you."

"Thank you for taking such good care of me. Under your touch, I feel cherished, loved even." My cheeks heat. "Not that I'm saying you love me or anything, just that— oh, God. Talk about ruining a good night."

I cover my face with my hands and contemplate sinking under the water to hide.

"Hey, no." Mateo pulls my hands away from my flaming cheeks. "Don't hide from me."

"I am so embarrassed."

"Why?" He truly sounds puzzled.

"Because I...I implied you love me!"

Just like in the parking lot at my father's funeral, he skims his index knuckle down beneath my jaw to my chin and tilts my gaze up to his. "Because I do—I *do* love you, *mariposita.*"

Slack-jawed, all I can do is stare.

"Aren't you going to say anything?" His lips tilt up into a teasing grin.

"I...you love me?" I search his eyes, looking for any hint of deception. But they're as open and honest as ever. "You really love me."

"*Sí*, I do."

I swallow roughly as happy tears wet my cheeks. "I love you, too."

His grin morphs into a megawatt smile. "Say it again."

"I love y—" He leans down and captures the end of my sentence in a hotly passionate kiss.

Water sloshes as he feasts upon my lips, our tongues slide together in a sensual dance until we have to break apart to breathe.

My chest is heaving and so is his.

"You relax," he tells me, rising to his feet, not even trying to hide his massive erection. "Your lips are too tempting and you need to rest."

"Where are you going?"

"To shower."

I sink down into the hot water, letting it lull me as I reflect on all that's happened not only tonight, but over the past couple of months.

Mateo turns the knob for the shower and steps under the spray. Unabashedly, I watch him, taking note of the way his sudsy hands move over his body. He's poetry in motion, taut and toned perfection, so much so that even something as banal as cleaning himself is mesmerizing.

Too bad for me, the show's over and he's wrapped in a towel before I can truly appreciate it.

"How do you feel?" he asks, running a smaller towel over his hair.

"Really good." My voice sounds sleepy to my own ears.

Mateo smiles. "I'll be right back with a towel."

He returns dressed in a pair of fresh boxers. "Let's get you back into my bed." He switches the lever to drain the tub before helping me up and out. I allow him to dry me off and lead me back into his bedroom, stark naked.

It's kind of crazy how comfortable I feel around him. But it's undeniable, too; something in him calls to something in me. Mateo Reyes feels like home.

"Are you ready for bed?" he asks right as a huge yawn escapes me. "I guess that is a yes."

I shrug. "What can I say? You wore me out."

A look of pure, masculine pride overtakes his features. "Damn straight. Now, let me get you a shirt."

"I packed pajamas."

"I want to see you in my shirt though." He crosses the room to his dresser and pulls out a threadbare t-shirt. "Arms up." I comply and he slides the shirt over my head. It's softer than silk and smells like him.

"Thank you."

"No need to thank me; everything I do for you is my pleasure."

I press up onto my tiptoes and kiss his cheek before getting into the bed.

Mateo crawls in after me, pulling me into his side so he's wrapped around me big-spoon style. "*Buenas noches, mariposita, te amo.*"

"Good night, Mateo, I love you, too."

I snuggle in deeper to his embrace, feeling lighter than I have in God knows how long, and within minutes, I'm lulled to sleep by the steady rhythm of his heart, knowing that right now, it's beating for me.

27

MATEO

THE FEELING OF SOFT, SUPPLE FLESH MOVING AGAINST MY own wakes me. Seraphine is curled into me with her head nestled into my chest, her arm around my middle, and one of her legs is hiked over my own.

In short—I'm in paradise.

She shifts, mumbling nonsense as she rubs her face against my chest. At some point during the night, her hair escaped the confines of her bun. Dark strands tickle my nose and hide her face from me.

I brush the wayward locks out of the way. She looks so completely at peace here in my bed; I don't want to move.

As gently as possible, I crane my neck to peek at the clock on my nightstand. It's half-past seven, making a good hour and a half later than I usually get up.

I'd lie here with her all day if I could. Lie here, love on her, make her come a few times, and then do it all over. Again, and again.

However, that's not an option, so I'll settle for the next best thing—waking her up with breakfast in bed.

It physically pains me to leave her—or maybe that's my morning wood aching—but I disentangle myself from her and roll to the edge of the bed. I linger for a moment, watching the steady rise and fall of her chest and press a kiss to her temple before heading to the kitchen and getting to work on breakfast.

After starting a pot of coffee, I realize it's our grocery day and the fridge is damn near empty—save for a takeout container of limoncello cheesecake.

Here's to hoping she doesn't mind sugar for breakfast.

I arrange a tray with two mugs of piping hot coffee, our sweet treat, and two spoons and head back to my room. She's still sound asleep. I place the tray at the end of the bed and perch on the edge near her.

"*Buenos días, mariposita*—wake up."

She hums softly and pulls the blanket over her head.

"I brought you breakfast."

"Coffee?" she asks, still buried beneath my comforter.

"Of course."

She sits up and pulls the blanket down. Her hair is a mess and I can't help but grin as I pass her mug to her. She inhales deeply before taking a sip. "Ooh, so good."

I join her fully on the bed, sitting with my back to the headboard and for a moment, we just exist together as we sip our coffees in the early quiet.

"How do you feel this morning?" I ask, hoping she gets my drift.

"Good; I feel really good."

"You're not sore?"

Her cheeks turn a sweet shade of pink. "I mean, not really."

My dick twitches. "Good."

Seraphine ducks her head and changes the subject. "You mentioned breakfast?"

Chuckling, I nod to the plate. "It's more like a really late—or early—dessert."

She passes me her mug and shucks the covers off. "Yum!"

Seraphine stretches forward, elongating her back and lifting her hips. The shirt I gave her to sleep in is bunched around her middle, giving me a jaw-dropping view of her delectable bare ass.

A low, sensual groan escapes me as my dick rises to the occasion. "Good enough to eat."

She glances back at me over her shoulder and flashes me a coy smile. "Then come get a bite," she whispers, bolder than I ever imagined her to be.

Coffee sloshes over the mug rims, but I couldn't care less. *Fuck.* How can I be expected to even form coherent thoughts with her wriggling her hips in the air, showing off her pretty pink pussy?

I lunge for her. Her position leaves her open and exposed perfectly for me, and like a man possessed, I bury my face between her legs and feast like she's my last meal.

After a handful of orgasms—for her, not me; I had some making up to do from last night—and a shower, Seraphine and I are curled up on the couch watching old episodes of *Roadkill*.

"The Draguar is the best," I argue, referring to the 1974 Jag they beat to hell and back on the show. "It did the most epic burnout!"

Seraphine scoffs but stays wrapped in my arms. "Puh-lease, the Rotsun is where it's at!"

"That clunker broke down constantly!"

"Well, duh." She laughs and it warms me from the inside out. "All of their cars either break down, overheat, or plain break! That's what makes it so good."

I nuzzle my nose into the top her head, breathing in her scent. "True, true."

The sound of the garage door opening has Seraphine tensing in my arms. "Shh, it's just Desi."

Seraphine cuts her eyes in the direction of the laundry room.

"She knows, and it—" is all I get out before my daughter bounds into the room.

"Ohhh, y'all look cozy," Desi says, plopping down into my chair.

I refuse to take her bait. "Did you have fun?"

"Yes! Renee's mom made homemade cinnamon rolls for breakfast; they were the s-h-i-t."

"Don't cuss," I reprimand her as Seraphine covers her smile with her hand.

"I didn't; I spelled it." Desi smirks, looking proud of her loophole.

"Smartass."

"Dad!" Desi feigns shock. "How could you use such language in the presence of ladies?"

Seraphine giggles, and I drop a kiss to the top of her head.

"What do you have going on today, *pollito*?"

Desi shrugs and trains her eyes on her lap.

"Talk to me," I urge her.

"I…it's just, um…"

The way she's bumbling around has my hackles raised. Des is the kind of kid who goes after what she wants wholeheartedly. I'm two seconds away from asking Seraphine to step out when she finally spits it out.

"I was hoping Seraphine would wanna hang today? Like…just me and her." Desi adds an apologetic shrug as she turns her eyes to the woman in question. "But it's cool if you're too busy."

Seraphine smiles wide, wiggling out of my hold. "I'm free all day—what did you have in mind?"

Desi perks up. "Really?"

"Heck yes. Girl time sounds like the perfect Saturday to me."

I grumble under my breath, pretending to be mad over not being included. Truthfully, I am ecstatic that two of the most important females in my life get along so well.

"Oh-em-gee! This is going to be the best day ever!"

"What did you have in mind?"

"Well, there's that new pottery place but we could get our nails done?"

Seraphine thinks on it for a few. "How about we do both?"

"Really?"

"Def. But, we gotta stop for food first. You people have nothing to eat here."

Desi grins. "It's grocery day."

Seraphine leans back into me. "Perfect. We can have a girls' day and your dad can grocery shop. It's a win-win."

"For who?" I ask, laughing.

Desi rolls her eyes. "Us, Dad. Duh."

SERAPHINE

"WHAT COLOR DO YOU WANT?" DESI ASKS, EYEING THE rows of nail polish before us.

"Hmm. I don't know."

She slants her eyes up at me. "Dad's favorite color is blue."

I breathe out a laugh. "And you think I should get blue for him?"

Desi shrugs. "I mean, I bet he'd like it."

"Are you picking your color for a boy?"

My teenage companion scoffs. "My only love is basketball—ooh! I'll get my team colors!"

"Good choice," I murmur, still taking in the colors, specifically the blues. Finally, I cave and ask, "What shade of blue?"

Triumphant, Desi reaches past me and grabs a bottle of pale shimmering blue-gray polish. "Like this."

I shake the bottle a few times before flipping it and reading the name out loud. "Check Out the Old Geysirs." I snort out a laugh, and so does Desi.

"Oh-em-gee!" she wheezes. "That is perfect. Because he's so old and you're not!"

"If you two could follow me," an employee says before I can reply. But her words loop in my mind while we get situated. "Would you ladies like anything to drink?"

We both order a soda and tell our respective nail techs what we'd like. Once they get started, I turn to Desi and word vomit all over her. "Are you okay with me and your dad being together? I know he *is* a lot older, and it's been just the two of y'all for a while. I really love your dad but your opinion matters, too, Desi. And I don't want you to ever think or worry that I'm trying to or even want to replace your mother. I know she is important and special and I promise to always try and honor her memory. And—"

"Spazaphine, chill."

"Did you just call me…Spaz…aphine?"

She snorts out a laugh, earning her a glare from her nail tech. "Stay still!"

"Sorry." She ducks her head. "And yeah, I did. You just went all crazy on me."

"Ugh." If my nails weren't being polished, I'd bury my face in my hands. "I guess I did."

"You love my dad?"

"You caught that, huh?"

Desi nods.

"Yeah, I love him."

"He loves you, too, you know?"

"What makes you so sure?"

"I just know. And I know you aren't trying to replace my mom. I wasn't ever worried about that. You're good people and you make my dad happy. He deserves to be happy. And as for the age thing—I'll tell you what I told him; it's just a number."

"You're a wise kid."

"Duh."

"You wanna get coffee before we go to the pottery place?"

"I will never turn down coffee."

"Same, girl. Same."

I pay for both of us once our nails are dry and then we walk the block to Dream Beans, chatting mindlessly as we go. We place our order and retreat to a small table near the front window.

"Can I ask you something?" Desi asks, toying with the straw of her drink.

"Always, anything."

She sucks down a sip of coffee. "Why did you leave the salon to work with my dad?"

"Well." It takes me a minute to gather my thoughts. "Total honesty? I kind of went off the rails after my dad died. I wasn't making very good choices."

"Like that night at the fair?"

"Yeah, like that night." A weary sigh leaves my lips. "You know, I don't think I ever thanked you for stepping in and helping me. You calling your dad"—a full body shiver runs through me— "saved me, in more ways than one."

Desi's eyes slide around the coffee shop before returning to me. "I could tell you weren't *you*. I couldn't leave you with *them*." She spits her last word with such acid, I can almost feel the burn.

"I mean it, Des. You and your dad saved me. I'll be grateful forever."

"There's a way you could repay me," she hedges.

"How's that?" I'm almost scared to hear her answer.

"You can love my dad. Treat him right; make him happy."

Tears cloud my vision. "I...I can definitely do that, Desi."

Her solemn face transforms to one of pure happiness. "Good. Now, let's go make some ugly vases."

Side-eyeing her, I say, "I don't know what you're talking about; my vase will be gorgeous."

I lied.

My vase looks more like an ashtray...that was left out in the sun and hit by a car...twice.

Desi's on the other hand is perfectly formed and she's not being a bit humble as she gloats.

"Look, don't feel bad, Spaz"—*yes, the nickname stuck*— "you did your best." She holds her department-store-worthy creation up like a trophy. "We can't all be artists."

"Yeah, yeah. Brag a little more."

"Um, hello? Of course, I'm gonna brag." She thrusts her vase toward me. "*Look!*"

"For real though, you're really talented, Des."

She beams. "Thanks. My mom was an artist, too. And Silvi! So, I guess it runs in the family, because what Dad does is art, too—just a different medium."

"Do you want to pursue art as a career?"

"Maybe. Big goals, I wanna play for the WNBA. But if that doesn't happen, I'd like to teach art or something. Or maybe run a place like this."

We hand our pieces over to the employee on duty so they can be fired in the kiln, with instructions to pick them on Friday.

As we walk back to the truck, my mind wanders to Desi's mom. She must have been a wonderful woman and while I'm not trying to replace her—not ever—I can't help but feel I have big shoes to fill.

"What kind of art do you like the most?" I ask as we approach the truck.

Desi answers once we're both buckled into our seats. "Well, before today, I would have said mixed media, but I think I really like sculpting, too."

"I don't know much about art, but I bet you could combine them."

She nods thoughtfully. "Maybe so."

"What kind of art did your mom do?"

"Oh, man, she was a painter—watercolor. Dad says her work was mostly abstract, but whenever I look at the pieces Dad saved, I always feel like there's something *more* to them. Does that make sense?"

"I think so. What about Silvi?"

"She paints too, but she prefers oil."

"That's really cool. I don't think I have an artistic bone in my body."

"Clearly." Desi snorts out a laugh, no doubt recalling my pathetic sculpting attempt. "But you know cars and you're really good at makeup."

"I'll give you the makeup thing; but trust me when I say, I know *about* cars. I get how they work and how to make them work. I do not know how to make them pretty."

"Whatever. Dad showed me pictures of Willow's Jeep. He said you helped paint it."

My cheeks heat recalling the other things we did in the paint booth. "Oh, um, yeah. Beginner's luck."

"Whatever. You gotta love yourself a little more, Spaz."

I pull the truck into the garage. "Yeah, maybe you're right."

Desi hops out before I'm fully into park. "Duh. I'm always right."

MATEO

I LEAN AGAINST THE DOORJAMB TO THE BATHROOM, watching as Seraphine twists her hair around some kind of curling iron. "You almost ready?" I ask, loving the way she's so at ease in my space.

Over the last month, she's spent more time here than at her place. Hell, she's one drawer away from being moved in. Which, if I'm being honest, I wouldn't mind.

"Almost." She wrinkles her nose and presses a hand to her belly. "Just gotta spray my hair and change."

"*Estás preciosa*—you look beautiful." I mean it, too. She's had this glow about her recently and it looks damn good on her.

"Thank you." She stands from the vanity stool and unplugs her iron. "Let me get dressed and we can go."

"Perfect. Let me go check on Desi."

Sure enough, my daughter is laid back on the couch, playing on her phone while she waits on us. "Time to go?" she asks.

"Just about."

"Cool. Can I drive?"

"Feels good outside; I figured we could walk."

Desi lifts one shoulder and then the other. "Yeah, a walk sounds nice."

I kick back into the seat beside her and discreetly glance down at her screen. She's thumbing through articles on the ESPN app, and not for the first time, I thank God for blessing me with such a good kid.

A few minutes later, Seraphine walks into the room. Her long legs are wrapped in a pair of leather leggings, and a thick cream sweater clings to her every curve. "Sorry I took so long."

"The end result is more than worth the wait, *mariposita*."

"Y'all are gross." Desi pretends to dry heave. "Let's go, *abuelita* promised me *rajas*."

"What's that?" Seraphine asks as we all walk toward the door.

"Girl!" Desi cries. "You're in for a treat. It's poblano peppers and onions and *crema* and so good. Just trust me."

"Sounds tasty. But I'm fairly certain anything Lety cooks is divine."

Seraphine and I walk hand-in-hand behind Desi, who is dribbling her basketball down the sidewalk.

"You think *Tío Arrón* will wanna pick up a game with me?"

I feign hurt. "Why only Arrón? I can play, too!"

Desi pivots around and passes the ball my way. I catch it effortlessly and check it back to her. "Fine, maybe we can all play."

"I might sit it out," Seraphine says. "I feel a little tired."

"Are you okay?" I ask, stopping midstride to check her over.

She tugs on my wrist until I start walking again. "I didn't sleep well, that's all."

"If you say so."

She nods. "I do."

We walk up to my mother's house right as Arrón pulls in on his motorcycle. He kills the engine and toes the kickstand down before stowing his helmet. "Desita! Rumor has y'all are undefeated this season?"

"Duh," she scoffs, as if her team's winning rank is a given.

"Congrats; I'm proud of you."

"Come to a game then," she says, passing him the ball.

He, too, catches it and bounces it back. "Consider it done."

Mamá opens the front door, greeting us warmly, before we even step foot on the porch. "*Hola, adelante, adelante*—hello, come in!"

We all stop and kiss her weathered cheeks before stepping into her home, but she pays Seraphine extra attention.

"I am glad you are here," Mamá tells Seraphine, clasping her hands.

Seraphine dips a shoulder. "I'm happy to be here. Thank you for asking me back after how I behaved last time."

Mamá releases Seraphine's hand and dusts her own together. "It was nothing. Come, let's eat."

The familiar scents of my mother's kitchen greet us as we venture past the threshold. I groan in appreciation.

"Smells good, huh?" I ask my beautiful date, but when I look her way, she looks a little green. I stop and turn her face toward mine. "Are you okay?"

Her brow dips but she forces a smile. "Yeah, just tired."

"Are you getting sick or something?"

Mamá chuckles as she sweeps past us. "Or something."

I wait until my mother is out of sight before asking, "Are you sure you're okay? Do we need to go?"

She laughs, but it sounds like a lie. "No, I'm good —promise."

I'm on the verge of calling her out when Silvi sticks her head out into the hall. "C'mon, everyone is waiting for you two!"

Seraphine tugs on my wrist, nodding toward my sister. "You heard her; let's go."

I relent and follow her into the kitchen.

The island is once again full of food. In addition to the *rajas*, there's also *pollo con mole, chicharron en salsa verde,* and *papas con chorizo*. In short, it's a feast fit for a king.

Unfortunately, Seraphine stills looks a little off. "How about you sit and I'll make you a small plate?" I ask, rubbing the small of her back in comforting strokes.

"Yes, please."

I lean in and kiss her lips, uncaring that we have an audience. "Anything for you."

A rosy blush blooms across her cheeks and she refuses to meet anyone's eyes as she slinks away to the table.

"Is she okay?" Silvi asks.

"Just tired."

Mamá snorts. "Not yet she isn't."

"What's that mean?"

"In time, Mate; in time."

With those cryptic words ringing in my ears, I make myself a plate with heaping portions of everything and Seraphine a plate of fruit along with some rice and tortillas.

I place hers in front of her on the table and claim the seat next to her.

She murmurs a softly spoken thanks between sips of water.

Mamá leads us in prayer and we all descend on our plates like starved vultures—with the exception of Seraphine, of course. She merely moves her food around with her fork.

She skips dessert as well, which is unfathomable since it's her famous *pay de límon*. Consisting of frozen layers of vanilla cookies and a sweet lemon sauce, it's as refreshing as it is tasty.

Once every plate has been all but licked clean, Desi announces it's time to play ball. Seraphine stays inside with Mamá. Which, if I'm being honest makes me a little nervous. I know she's in good hands—they just happen to be very nosy, meddling hands as well.

We play two-on-two—Desi and Silvi against Arrón and me—and while Silvi isn't too athletic, Desi more than makes up for it.

"So, it's serious?" my sister asks, half-ass guarding me while I dribble the ball.

"What is?"

She shoulder checks me.

"Foul!" I cry, but no one cares.

"You and Seraphine," Arrón answers for her.

Desi steals the ball and shoots. "Duh, they're like, in love." The ball swishes through, nothing but net.

"Oh, it's like that?" Silvi asks, as Arrón takes the ball and checks it to me.

I shoot the ball, but it bounces off the rim, right into Desi's hands. "Yeah, it's like that."

My siblings exchange a look before breaking out into matching grins.

"Good," my brother says, "I really like her."

Silvi nods. "I think Imani would like her, too."

We all fall quiet at the mention of my late wife. A peace thrums deep within and I know they're right.

Choked with emotion, all I can do is nod.

Desi manages to score again while I'm lost in my feelings, making her and Silvi the winners, leading us twenty to fourteen.

"Play again?" my daughter asks, not even sounding out of breath.

"I'm gonna go check on Seraphine, y'all have at it."

"Horse?" she asks her aunt and uncle as I head back into the house.

I find Seraphine in the living room. She's out cold on the couch, sleeping deeply. I guess she really was tired.

Mamá is in the kitchen, washing dishes.

"Let me help you," I say, nudging her aside so I can take over. "You cooked, the least I can do is clean up."

She dries her hands and pats my cheek. "You're a good boy, Mate."

"I'm a man, Mamá."

She clucks her tongue at me. "You will always be my boy."

"Yeah, yeah."

"I packed some leftovers for you; make sure Seraphine gets some."

"Of course."

"You need to make sure she is eating well."

My eyes slide from the sudsy, dish-filled water to my mother. "She is a grown woman who can feed herself."

"Ouch!" I rub the back of my head. "Why did you just smack me with the dish towel?"

"Open your eyes, Mate, and *see*! Take care of her."

I feel like she's saying one thing and meaning another. Unfortunately for both of us, her hidden message is lost on me.

SERAPHINE

"Are you sure you're okay to go to the party today?" Mateo asks for what feels like the hundredth time.

"I'm not missing my niece's birthday party." I mulishly cross my arms over my chest.

"You're not still tired? You were so puny last night at my mother's—I'm worried."

I shake my head no, but a yawn betrays me.

"We can both stay?" he offers, but I won't be swayed and he sees in the defiant tilt of my chin. "Fine. But if you feel worse, I'm taking you home."

"I'll be fine," I grumble, "now let's go or we'll be late."

"If you say so." Mateo eyes me long and hard. "Let me load up the Jeep."

I follow him outside in case he needs help. But the sight before me is so comical, all I can do is laugh.

"You like?"

He has a trailer hitched to his truck with the sparkly pink Jeep—along with a trailer of its own—ratcheted down in the center.

"I love."

"Me?" He smirks. "I know. I love you, too."

"C'mon, Casanova."

We get a lot of honks and waves on the drive out to Magnolia's. People are loving the pint-sized custom ride we're hauling. If the reactions of this many strangers are anything to go by, Willow will absolutely flip for the thing.

Simon meets us in the drive and lets out a low whistle. "Now that's a damn Powerwheel."

"It's nice, right?" Mateo asks, pulling him into one of those weird back-slapping man hugs.

"Nicer than nice."

"Sweet. Help me get it around back?"

"You got it."

While they set to work unloading the Jeep, I grab our gift—a Willow-sized racing helmet, painted to match her new ride—from the back seat.

Magnolia meets me at the door with a warm hug. "I've missed you!"

"Miss you, too. Where should I put this?"

"I've got it." She takes the box from me and carries it out back, where the party is already in full swing. Luckily, they rented an inflatable bounce house, so the kids don't even notice Simon and Mateo wheeling the Jeep back.

"Mags, you're out of spinach dip—Seraphine, you're here!" Azalea wraps me in a hug.

"There's more in the fridge."

"On it!" Azalea bounds off into the house.

"Let's catch up." Magnolia leads me over to a set of chairs. "How are things?"

"Which things?"

She nods her head toward Mateo.

"Oh, those things. They're good...*really* good."

"Like, *in love* good?"

"Who's in love?" Myla Rose asks, pulling up a chair to join us.

I raise my hand slightly. "Me. I am."

Myla Rose squeals and scoots her chair even closer. "Since when?"

Shrugging, I confess, "I don't know; it just sort of happened."

"What did?" Azalea asks, perching on the arm of Myla's chair.

"Seraphine is in love with Mateo."

Azalea rolls her eyes. "Duh. Old news."

We all turn to look at her.

"What do you mean?" I ask, wondering how she could've known—especially when she was so damn blind at the start of her own relationship.

"Girl." She shakes her head. "The way you look at that man, he may as well have hung the moon."

"He's pretty amazing."

"The real question is," Myla Rose says, leaning forward, "is it mutual?"

I can feel myself smiling. "Yeah, it is."

"Who said it first?" Magnolia asks.

"Uh. Well. I almost said it and then felt really stupid, so he said it and yeah..."

My three friends squeal before congratulating me.

"Sorry to break up girl talk," Simon says, "but it's time for cake."

Magnolia smiles up at him with a gaze full of love; I

can't help but wonder if that's the look Azalea was talking about?

We all move to the back of the deck where they have the cake set up. Mateo meanders over to me, wrapping me in his arms for all to see.

"You look happy," he murmurs against my neck before kissing me there.

"I am." I look up at him over my shoulder. "How could I not be?"

A chorus of the *Happy Birthday* song starts up before I can reply and Willow blows out her candles like a champ. "Pwesents first?" she asks, puppy eyes and all, and like the sucker my cousin is, Magnolia agrees.

"Sure, Wills, presents first."

At some point, the guys covered the Jeep with a tarp, so sweet Willow hasn't even noticed its existence.

She tears through package after package like a tiny tornado—one with manners though, as she pauses long enough to thank each gift giver before moving on to the next.

Luckily, the helmet from Mateo and me is toward the back of the pile and is the last gift she opens. Even without knowing what it is for, the pink sparkles have her *oohing* and *ahhing* before jamming it onto her head.

"Wook, Daddy! I go fast!" She runs toward Simon and leaps into his arms.

"Hell yes, you do," he croons.

"Dat's a bad word."

"My bad," he mutters, the tips of his ears turning pink. "Wanna open your last present?"

Her eyes widen comically. "There's more?"

"Yeah." He tips his head toward the big, blue tarp. "Go and take a peek underneath that."

She races over and instead of pulling the tarp off, she scoots under. "Whoa!"

"Do you like it?" Simon asks.

Willow crawls back out. "I dunno. It was too dark to see."

All of the party-goers chuckle and Simon whips the tarp off with the flair of a magician removing a tablecloth.

Her little jaw drops as she releases an ear-splitting squeal. "I wove it! I wove-wove-wove it!" She hugs Simon and Magnolia before clamoring into her Jeep. "Can I dwive it?"

"How about cake first?" Magnolia asks. Willow responds by pursing her lips together and making engine sounds. "Fine, speed demon, take a lap or two."

Simon and the other guys all head off to watch Willow test out her new toy while Magnolia divvies up the cake.

I eagerly accept my plate, knowing she had it made by Sprinkles—A.K.A. the best cake shop in the whole damn county.

I fork up a bite heavy with icing and bring it to my lips only to gag. I slap a hand over my mouth and toss my plate down before running inside the house to the bathroom.

My eyes water as acid crawls up my throat. I slam open the door to the hall bath and hit my knees before the toilet right as everything in my stomach comes back up.

Footsteps sound from somewhere in the house, but I'm too exhausted to care.

"Seraphine," Magnolia calls my name from the other side of the door.

All I can manage is a garbled moan in response as another wave of nausea hits me.

"Are you okay?"

The feeling passes and I offer a weak, "Yeah."

"We're coming in."

Of course, they're all here.

The moderately sized bathroom feels a lot smaller with all four of us in it.

"Are you okay?" Mags asks.

With my head resting on the toilet seat, I nod.

"Ugh." Azalea gags. "Sit up."

I do and she slams the lid and flushes.

"What's going on?" Myla Rose asks, running the hand towel under the faucet. She passes it to me and I press it to the back of my neck.

"I don't—the cake—I don't know."

"Girl, the cake was fine," Azalea says.

Myla gets a worried look in her eyes. "Seraphine, is there any chance you could be pregnant?"

My initial reaction is to deny it, but—that first time Mateo and I slept together, we didn't use a condom.

Surely, I'm not...

"I have a few tests at home, let me run and grab one," Myla Rose says, slipping from the bathroom before any of us can object. Though, I guess I'd be the only one to actually object.

Since she lives next door, she is back in a flash. She slides the test from her purse and hands it to me. "We'll be right outside, okay?"

"Yeah, sure. Okay." They all start to file out when a thought hits me. "Wait! Aren't you supposed to do this in the morning or something?"

Myles smiles at me. "Just go ahead and do it, 'kay?"

Gulping, I nod.

It takes me a few minutes to work up the courage—as well as the need to pee. During that time, I swish my mouth out with water, wash my hands, and thoroughly read the instructions.

Finally, all that's left is to do it. I pee on the stick, recap it, and place it facedown before flushing and washing my hands yet again.

The second they hear the flush, all three come filing back in.

"Well?" Azalea asks.

"It said to wait three minutes," I whisper.

Ever the girl scout, Myla Rose flips her phone around so we can see the screen. "I started the time when I heard the flush."

We fall silent while we wait for the alarm. When it dings, I nearly jump out of my skin.

"Flip it over," Azalea urges.

I suck in a big breath and slowly release it before turning over the little stick. Sure enough, two dark pink lines greet me.

Holy. Shit. "I'm—"

"Pregnant," Magnolia finishes my sentence.

"What are you gonna do?" Azalea asks.

"What do you mean?"

"Abortion? Adoption? Mom up?"

Her words hit me square in the chest. While I absolutely believe every woman has the right to choose, I know immediately that I am keeping this baby. "I'm gonna be a mom," I whisper, a million different conflicting emotions clogging my throat.

Like the ride-or-dies they are, all three of my friends wrap me in a hug.

"I'm really happy for you," Magnolia says, her cheeks wet with tears.

"Me, too," Myla Rose echoes her sentiment. "Motherhood is one hell of a journey, but it's also the most amazing journey. You got this, girl."

"Yeah, happy-joy-joy," Azalea, lightening the mood with her particular brand of snark, "but how are you gonna tell Mateo?"

MATEO

I'M SWITCHING A LOAD OF LAUNDRY—SHOP RAGS—WHEN MY cell phone buzzes in my pocket. As lame as it may sound, I'm hoping it's Seraphine.

Last night, after Willow's party wound down, Myla Rose declared the womenfolk needed a slumber party, and while I'm always happy to see Seraphine spend time with those she loves and who love her, my bed felt empty last night without her in it.

After tossing the last of the rags into the dryer, shutting the door, and hitting start, I slide my phone from my pocket. My lips curve into a smile at the sight of her name.

Seraphine: Can we talk?

Worry slides in, crowding my earlier happiness against the wall.

Me: Always. What's up?

Seraphine: In person?
Me: You never need to ask. Where are you?
Seraphine: On your porch.

I shove my phone back into my pocket and fly to the door. Sure enough, there on the other side of it, is Seraphine looking a little worse for wear.

"Come inside." I haul her into the house and into my arms, holding her close. I'm not sure what's up, but she's clearly upset. Her downturned lips, watery eyes, and curved shoulders have me going into *knight-mode*, ready to slay her dragons. "Are you okay?"

She steps out of my embrace and wraps her arms around her middle. "Can we sit?"

"Of course."

In the living room, she heads for the couch, but I pull her onto my lap in my chair. For a minute, she sits there, her back ramrod straight before finally melting into me.

"Talk to me, *mariposita.*"

She inhales a wobbly breath. "You said we'd be okay, no matter what, right?"

Instantly, I'm on high alert. "Yeah." I rub my hands over her back, trying to loosen the tightly bunched muscles.

"And you meant it?" She looks up at me with tired eyes.

"Wholeheartedly," I assure her.

She thinks for a moment before nodding to herself. "I'm pregnant."

My hands still. Time stills. The entire fucking earth comes to a screeching halt on its axis—or at least my world did. "Pregnant?" I rasp.

Seraphine nods, tears dripping from her chin.

"Un don de Dios." I cup her jaw and tilt her face to mine, swiping away her tears with my thumbs. "We're going to have a baby?"

"Are you upset?" The look of sheer agony on her face as she waits for my response has my heart beating a staccato rhythm in my chest.

I shake my head. "This baby—*our* baby—is a gift from God."

She sniffles. "You mean it?"

Words fail me, so I answer her the only way that feels right—with a kiss. The taste of her tears mingles with something inherently Seraphine as I lick into her mouth. Our tongues slide together, my hands settling reverently on her belly.

"I love you," I whisper, my lips still moving against hers. "I love you and our baby."

Seraphine whimpers, but I swallow the sound, deepening our kiss. She pulls away and braces herself with her hands on my shoulders, looking me solidly in the eyes. "I love you, too, Mateo. I…I want this, with you. I need you to know that."

Grinning like a fool, I slide my hands around from her belly to her ass and stand.

"Wha-where are we going?"

"To celebrate," I growl as I carry her back to the bedroom, placing her on her feet near the foot of the bed. Even though Desi isn't home, I shut and lock the door.

Seraphine watches me, an unreadable look on her face, as I prowl the length of floor in front of her like a wild animal.

"This is a weird celebration," she murmurs, humor lacing her tone.

I whip around to face her and fall to my knees. Sliding my hands beneath the material of her shirt, I press a kiss to her stomach, right below her navel.

"I need to calm myself before touching you," I confess. I pepper her entire belly with kisses, each one a little hotter than the last. "You're going to have my child—knowledge like that does something to a man, *mariposita.*"

"Oh, yeah? What's that?"

I can't decide if she's being coy or oblivious. Either way, I rise to my full height and grab her hand, pressing it against my erection.

"Oh," comes her breathy reply. "Really?"

"Really."

She squeezes my dick through my sweats and I shamelessly rock into her hand.

"I need you," I groan.

"I'm here, always." She releases me and steps away, her words at odds with her actions, until she begins peeling away her clothing until she's standing completely and totally naked before me. "Have me, Mateo."

My eyes eat her up, blazing a path that my hands eagerly follow. I trace my fingers over her collarbones, down to her perfect breasts.

She moans at the slightest of contact and before I can think better of it, I lean in and draw her achingly sensitive nipple into my mouth. I lick and suck as she digs her nails into my shoulders and wiggles her hips.

"Feels so good, Mateo, but I need more."

I drop back down to my knees, kissing my way down her belly before spreading her pussy lips with my thumbs.

She's already wet and ready for me when I dart my tongue out to lick her slit.

"Fuck," she grinds out. Her legs wobble as I make contact with her clit, swirling my tongue against the sensitized flesh. "Yes!" She tugs on my hair—*hard.* "Wait, no!"

I pull back and look up at her. "What's wrong?" I ask, wiping the back of my hand over my lips.

"I can't wait, I need you to fuck me."

My lips lift into a faint but indulgent smile as I stand. I pull my shirt over my head, tossing it to the floor, before pushing my sweats down my hips and stepping out of them.

Seraphine reaches for me, but I stop her, pinning both of her wrists to her belly. "Not yet."

She whimpers softly, as desperate for my touch as I am for hers.

I release her and move past her, crawling onto the bed. I prop myself against the headboard, never once breaking eye contact, even as I stroke my hard length.

"Come here," I say and she obliges. "Closer." I pat my lap and she straddles me. "Now listen closely, *mariposita.* I'm not going to fuck you."

She parts her lips, no doubt to tell me off, but I lean forward and push my tongue into her mouth, kissing her hard until she's rocking her hips, sliding her wet pussy against my rock-hard cock.

"Please," she pants, "stop teasing me and fuck me."

I shake my head back and forth, all the while helping her seat herself on my dick. We both groan as she lowers herself all the way down. "I'm not going to fuck you after you tell me we're having a baby. No. I'm going to make love to you."

Her lashes flutter as she rolls her hips in a figure-eight motion, damn near driving me wild.

We move together in complete harmony, meeting one another kiss for kiss, touch for touch, and thrust for thrust until we're both on the brink of release.

But I need more. I'm not ready for this to end.

Pitching up, I roll us over, pressing our hands into the mattress over Seraphine's head.

Seraphine stretches beneath me, canting her head to grant me access to the sweet spot between her neck and shoulders. I slide my lips over her sweat-slicked skin, murmuring how much I love her between open-mouthed kisses.

She wraps her legs around my waist, locking her ankles together, allowing me to hit that spot deep inside her.

"Fuck, yes." I grind against her clit on every down-stroke, making her clench around me. "I can't believe you're mine."

With a trembling hand, she reaches up and cups my cheek. *"Te amo."*

Hearing her confess her love for me in my native language does all kinds of things to me.

"Me siento muy bien cuando estoy contigo—I feel so good when I am with you," I groan, raising up so I can see the pleasure playing out on her beautiful face.

She sucks her lower lip into her mouth, panting hard.

"This is forever—*we* are forever, *mariposita.*" I thrust into her, palming her belly with my hands.

"Yes-yes-yes, always." She lifts her hips, meeting me thrust-for-thrust.

The feeling of her pulsing around me is more than I take. "Come for me," I murmur, pinching her clit hard enough to send her screaming over the edge, with me right behind her.

It pains me to pull out of Seraphine, but I do. My body instantly misses the heat of hers.

And judging from the small whimper as I roll to lie beside her, she's mourning the loss of contact, too.

"You good?" I murmur, stroking her hair away from her face.

She blinks. "I was nervous to tell you. Like, really nervous. I wasn't really...I don't know what I was expecting to be honest. But it definitely wasn't jubilant happiness and a few orgasms—not that I'm complaining."

I can't help but grin at her stammering reply. "We should celebrate!"

Seraphine rolls to face me. "Pretty sure my thighs are still sticky from our *celebration*."

Her unexpected response pulls a laugh from deep within me. "No, let's go out and celebrate."

"Really?"

"*Sí, mariposita.* Get up!" I toss off the covers and spring to my feet.

She grumbles and groans as she hauls herself out of the bed, mumbling under her breath something about a nap. "Sure, where?"

"Anywhere you want to go. Are you craving—wait, too soon for that." I shake my head. "You'd think I'd remember, but it's been a *long* time."

"Definitely no cravings yet. It's still really early."

My gut sinks. "*Dios mío!* I never even asked how far

221

along you were, the due date, doctors'
appointments, *nada!*"

"Hey." Seraphine cups my cheek. "We got a little swept
away. It's okay."

"So, how far along are you?"

"It's still really early—I'm only four weeks."

My gaze dips to her belly, already imagining it
swollen. "It's so crazy to think you have our baby inside of
you. What about the doctor?"

"I plan on calling my doctor tomorrow, but Myla Rose
says they probably won't want to see me until I'm eight or
so weeks."

I bolt upright as a sense of urgency races through me.
"I want to come to every appointment. Will you let me?"

"Of course—this is your baby, too, Mateo."

Instantly, relief blankets me. "Thank you."

"Were you as involved with Desi?"

"No." Remorse weights my every word. "I was trying
to get my shop up and running and did not prioritize the
way I should have. I made it to the big appointments and
her birth, but that's it."

Seraphine sits up, drawing my gaze down to hers.
"Don't beat yourself up over it. You're only human."

"It's just something I've always regretted." It's also why
I make such an effort to be involved in her life now. Sure,
Desi doesn't know I didn't attend her pre-natal appointments, and maybe my guilt is misplaced, but it exists in
me all the same.

"We all have regrets. Like I said—human. But the thing
about being human is, we have the potential to learn and
grow, to do better, and trust me when I say that you're
one of the best."

Her praise makes me feel about ten feet tall. "The best you say?" I lean in and nuzzle her neck.

"Don't fish for compliments—it's not becoming."

I chuckle at her unwitting remark. "Pretty sure there's a joke in there somewhere, *mariposita*."

"And I'm pretty sure you offered to take me out to celebrate."

"That I did. Let's get cleaned up."

SERAPHINE

"You're sure you're okay spending the day with my mom?" Mateo asks, passing me a cup of hot cocoa—because apparently the smell of coffee makes me want to hurl now, along with pretty much everything else I love.

"Desi is coming with her, but even if she weren't, I would be fine with it." I take a sip of my chocolatey drink, letting it warm me from the inside. "I love your mother." I mean it too; ever since that last dinner at Lety's, we've taken to texting every day.

Mateo chuckles. "She loves you too."

"We need to tell her—and Desi—about the baby. I'm almost twelve weeks and if you look close enough, you can tell it's not just bloating."

"You look incredible," Mateo growls. He's made it more than clear he loves every extra pound on me.

"I look like I did five trips to the buffet. My jeans are getting a little snug."

He rolls his eyes; I lift my top and point to the hair-tie securing my pants.

"We really do need to tell them. Ideas?" I ask, like I haven't been scouring the internet for ideas.

"I've heard the words *I'm pregnant* are pretty effective."

"Smartass," I mutter under my breath.

"You love it." He wags his eyebrows.

"I love you."

Growing serious, he sets his mug on the counter and cups my cheek. "I love you too, and we can tell them however and whenever you want. You could even do it today."

"Really?"

"Really. If it makes you happy, it makes me happy, *mariposita.*"

"Okay, good."

"What do y'all have planned today?"

I bounce on my toes as a beaming smile splits my cheeks. "We're doing a floral arrangement class at Stems and then getting lunch at Dilly's."

Mateo steps into me, kissing my temple. "Maybe I can meet y'all for lunch and we can tell her then?"

I pop up and kiss his lips. "That's perfect!"

"You want me to drop you off then? That way we can take one car home?"

"Are you sure you don't mind?"

Mateo stares at me blankly. "Are you really asking if I *mind* spending more time with you?"

"You got me there." I kiss him one more time before chugging down the rest of my cocoa. "Now, let's go so we aren't late."

"In such a hurry to get rid of me." He shakes his head in mock-disappointment. "You wound me."

I roll my eyes at his antics while rinsing my mug.

"Come on Seraphine." He tugs on the hood of my jacket. "You're gonna make us late."

Laughter bubbles up inside me, spilling out. "You're crazy, you know that?"

"Crazy for you."

Mateo gets a call from his brother the second we pull out of the garage, so I spend the quick drive to Stems on my phone pinning *more* cute pregnancy announcements.

I give him a quick kiss on the cheek when he pulls into the parking lot before hopping out of the truck. "Love you," I holler as he pulls away, blowing a kiss.

He blows one back in the rearview mirror.

I trek inside, eager to escape the cold. Ever prompt, I find Lety and Desi already waiting for me.

Desi spots me first and flies over to hug me. "I didn't think you'd ever get here. She keeps asking me about boys!" she mutters the last part so only I can hear it.

"I'm perfectly on time."

Desi rolls her eyes in agitation, but a smile breaks free

"Seraphine!" Lety wraps me in a tight hug, kissing each cheek. As she releases me, I swear, she glances down meaningfully at my stomach. "You are looking well. Glowing."

"Oh, thanks. Um, you look well too?"

Both Lety and Desi laugh at my less-than-eloquent reply. "Come, let's arrange flowers."

The class is intimate, with only five other people plus the instructor.

"Good morning," a chipper redhead says. "I'm Toni and I'll be teaching y'all how to make one helluva bouquet today. If you'll move over to our worktable, we can get started."

We all shuffle to the massive table in the back of the shop. Desi gets paired with another girl close to her age, and the two become fast friends.

"Please make sure your workspace has all of the following—a vase, shears, a thorn stripper, a bottle of water, a packet of soluble preservative, and tape."

Once Toni is satisfied that we all have the required equipment, she moves on. "Perfect. In groups of two, moving from left to right, we're going to take turns selecting our flowers. Please select anywhere from two-six types. Think out of the box—mix it up, be bold, and don't forget your greenery!"

Lety and I are last to go.

I gravitate toward brighter blooms—gorgeous orange lilies, red and orange carnations, purple chrysanthemums, along with orange miniature carnations.

Lety on the other hand goes for ruby red roses and sunflowers.

"You need something green," she tells me, assessing my selections. "Perhaps some baby's breath?"

I'm sure it's my imagination, but it feels like she emphasized the word baby—*no, that's crazy.* "I was thinking about these oak leaves."

Her eyes dart to my stomach again. "I suppose."

We head back to the table and Toni dives right into what we need to do to build our arrangements.

"First things first, ladies, we're going to cut our stems at an angle—but please be sure to keep them one-and-a-half times taller than your vases. Once you're done, please remove any thorns or leaves that will sit below the water line. This is important because it helps stop bacteria growth, thus extending the longevity of your flowers."

Toni falls quiet as we follow her instructions, snipped and measuring and chatting quietly amongst ourselves.

As we're working, a bitter metallic taste fills my mouth. Lety must see my disgust on my face. "Are you okay?" she asks.

I push my tongue against the roof of my mouth, trying to hold back the sick feeling the taste is causing. "Yeah, just, I don't know—a bad taste—but I'll be fine."

She eyes me curiously. "You need water. And a mint." She bends and retrieve a peppermint from her bag, passing it to me. Before I can thank her, she's bustling over to Toni in search of water.

The mint instantly reduces the coppery taste, making me sigh in relief.

I can't make out their conversation, but Lety speaks urgently, glancing back to me several times. Whatever she said has Toni leaving her post at the head of the table.

The gorgeous florist returns moments later with a bottle of water and a kind smile.

"Thank you," I murmur to Lety as she presses the ice-cold bottle into my hands. After glugging down a few sips, I feel almost as good as new.

"You are welcome. It happened to me too."

"What did?" I ask, resuming my leaf removal.

"My mouth always tasted like I was sucking on pennies when I was pregnant."

"What?" Desi shouts, obviously tuned into our conversation. "You're pregnant?"

The scissors fall from my hands, clattering onto the table, as I jerk to a halt mid cut. "I... uh... sorry, what?"

Lety gives me a look that's equal parts pity and understanding. "Pregnant. You are with child, yes?"

"Are you really?" Desi's eyes are wider than dinner plates. "Oh, my God! Does Dad know?"

My throat feels like sandpaper as it works overtime for me to swallow. "Yes," I whisper, answering them both, right as Toni jumps back into directing us through the art of floral arrangement.

"Everyone please pour the provided water into your vase, followed by the preservative."

"This conversation is not over," Lety whispers from the side of her mouth, her words a soft promise rather than a threat.

Regardless, worry winds through me like a snake on a limb, constricting around my heart.

"Start with your largest flowers first. Work in a circle and rotate the vase as you go. Keep an eye on your symmetry. Wash, rinse, and repeat until your arrangement is complete."

I sneak a peek a Desi while she works; her cheeks are pink and her eyes are bright, but otherwise, her face is unreadable.

Lety hums *Rockabye Baby* under her breath as she works.

I tug at the neckline of my sweater.

"Are you good?" she asks.

"Yeah, just hot."

Lety spins her vase around, checking it from all angles before nodding once. "It is increased blood flow."

"What?"

"You are hot from increased blood flow."

"Oh," I reply, dumbfounded.

I try and get lost in my work, but I'm pretty sure my

bouquet looks like it came from the dollar-store-discount-bin.

"Time to go, Seraphine," Lety says, startling me.

Sure enough, everyone around us is packing up to go. I quickly neaten my station and grab my vase. "Are you, um, good with Dilly's still? I asked Mateo if he wanted to meet us there."

"Desi has me hooked on the place," she says, pulling her granddaughter into her side.

"Yeah, it's good."

"Good?" Desi cries. "Their grilled cheeses are lit!"

I nod in agreement, but I'm a million miles away.

Desi calls shotgun, and I'm all too happy to hideout in the backseat and watch over our flower arrangements.

The second the engine turns over and the doors lock, my anxiety ramps up to a whole new level and I find myself desperate to explain. "We were planning to tell you —today actually."

"I have known for a long time," Lety says.

"What? Did Mateo tell you?" Hurt pinches my heart. I mean, I wouldn't fault him for telling her, I just wish he would have clued me in.

"No." She parallel parks in front of Dilly's like a boss.

"Then how do you—"

"A mother just knows." Lety kills the engine. "This baby is a good thing. A blessing. I am excited. Let's celebrate."

"Now?"

Desi clambers out of the car, with Lety hot on her heels. I rush to follow. "Yes! Now!" the younger Reyes crows.

Her grandmother grins conspiratorially. "Cake—we will order cake!"

I loop my arms through theirs. "I do like cake."

MATEO

I walk to my truck with a spring in my step and an anticipatory smile on my face. I've got a plan in place and all that's left to nail down is the timing.

But before I can figure out any of that, I've got lunch plans and a different kind of bomb to drop.

Though, I guess bomb isn't really the right word—unless it's a confetti bomb or something—because I know without a doubt Mamá is going to be happy.

Ecstatic even.

She's been wanting more grandkids since Desi was born.

Something tells me Des is going to be on board as well.

The whole way to Dilly's my mind bounces back-and-forth between the baby and the *other* thing. I'm ninety percent confident, but damn if that ten percent doesn't freak me out.

"One thing at a time," I murmur to myself as I park across the street.

A small smile unfurls when I walk past my mother's

perfectly parked car. Swear, the woman parallel parks with robot-like precision.

I step into Dilly's and instantly find Mamá, Desi, and Seraphine at a table toward the back. My daughter and my mother are seated facing me; they're talking, laughing, and carrying on like they've known Seraphine forever.

The sight of it warms my heart.

Mamá sees me approaching; she nudges Desi but says nothing.

"Hopefully I didn't keep y'all waiting," I say, dropping my hands onto Seraphine's shoulders.

She jumps and twists around in her seat. "Oh, my God! You snuck up on me."

"I'm sorry," I murmur. "What's got y'all giggling like schoolgirls?"

Seraphine starts to reply, but Mamá speaks over her, eyes twinkling with mischief. "We were discussing wedding plans, *mijo*."

Desi slaps a hand over her mouth to hold in her laughter while Seraphine looks distraught.

"Wha?" she twists back to face my mother so fast I think even *I* have whiplash.

Mamá shrugs innocently. "Wouldn't a Christmas wedding be nice?"

"Oooh, yes!" Desi agrees. "We could do a cocoa bar!"

Seraphine slumps forward, covering her face with her hands. "Mateo," she cries my name. "I swear, we we're *not* talking about wedding plans!"

As an internal debate wages within be me, I pat my pocket and decide to go for broke. "Do not hide from me, Seraphine."

"I'm not hiding," she says—clearly hiding. "I'm just—"

"Turn around," I tell her, sliding the velvet box from my pocket as I drop down to one knee. "Turn around so I can ask you to be my wife."

"What?"

From the corner of my eye, I notice Desi is filming the whole thing while Mamá texts furiously, no doubt texting my *tía* Sofia.

"Turn around so I can tell you that I want to start and end each day with you at my side."

"Is this real?" Her voice quavers.

"Turn around, *mariposita,*" I urge her. "Turn around and find out."

"Yeah, Spaz! Turn around already!"

In what feels like slow motion, Seraphine turns toward me. "Mateo," she whispers.

"Marry me?"

Her mouth opens and closes a few times, but no words ever come out.

"Marry me and make me the happiest man on the planet."

"Are you…are you serious right now?"

"Do I look serious?" I pop the lid on the ring box, revealing the blinding diamond nestled in a twisted halo rose gold setting. "I never thought I would get a second chance at the kind of happiness you've brought into my life—much less at love. Say yes—make us a family, take my name, you already have my heart."

Random patrons yell for her to say yes, but Seraphine is frozen with tears streaming down her cheeks.

Finally, after what feels like eons, she nods.

"Yes? Is that a yes? I need to hear the words, *mariposita.*"

"Yes, of course. I love you, yes!"

EPILOGUE – SERAPHINE

Sucking in a sharp breath, I pause in the doorway, letting Desi and Magnolia trail ahead of me.

Lety's backyard looks like a winter wonderland. Rows of string lights twinkle overhead, casting a magical glow. There's garland, crimson ribbons, and twinkling lights wrapped around the deck rails and poinsettias line the steps leading down into the grass.

Prettier still is the huge wreath suspended between two shepherd's hooks under the pergola in the yard.

But the most catching sight of all is Mateo standing under the wreath in a pitch-black suit with the most handsome lopsided grin on his face. Simon and Arrón stand with him.

Mateo stands up straighter the second he spots me. His eyes lock onto me, tracking my every movement.

My heart pitter-patters in a flurry of nerves and excitement as the first chords of Twenty-One Pilot's rendition of "Can't Help Falling in Love" trickles through the outdoor speakers.

I clutch my bouquet to my chest as the weight of the moment barrels into me like a freight train.

Like most little girls, I envisioned my father walking me down the aisle, but he isn't here to do that. And while it took me a long time to come to terms with his death, I know he's here in my heart and in spirit.

I also know he would undoubtedly bless this union, so when my groom beckons me to him with a crook of his finger, I don't hesitate.

Not for one single second.

It takes every ounce of self-control I posses to not sprint down the aisle.

"*Te ves hermosa esta noche, mariposita*—you look beautiful tonight," Mateo murmurs once I'm standing before him.

"You do too." My chest heaves in anticipation.

Mateo strokes my cheek tenderly before stepping back so the officiant can begin.

The officiant clears his throat. "Family and friends, we are gathered here today to celebrate the uniting of two hearts. Tonight, we will witness the joining of Mateo Reyes and Seraphine Reynolds in marriage. If there is anyone present who has just cause why this couple should not be united, let them speak now or forever hold their peace."

He pauses. When no one speaks, he continues, leading us through the questions of consent and into our vows— which we opted to write ourselves.

"Seraphine, *Dios me dio una segunda oportunidad contigo y no la voy a desaprovechar. Eres mi corazon, mi alma, mi luna y mi sol. Te voy a respetar y a cuidar y voy a crecer contigo en las buenas y en las malas, como tu amigo, amante y compañero.*

Si yo alguna vez pense que eras fragil como las alas de una mariposa, estaba equivocado. Eres fuerte y hermosa y agraciada y no puedo esperar a pasar el resto de mi vida contigo amándote."

I sway toward him slightly as the rumble of his deep, accented voice rolls over me. "I don't have a clue of what you just said, but whatever it was, I love you and I absolutely take you as my husband."

Mateo fights a grin as the officiant leans down and whispers, "Not quite there yet, my dear."

"Oh." I duck my head. "Oops. Sorry."

"Do not apologize, *mariposita*," Mateo says, skimming a knuckle along my jaw.

More than anything, I want to plant my lips on his; but we're *definitely not* to that part of the ceremony.

"What I said was, God has given me a second chance with you, and I will not waste it. You are my heart, my soul, my sun, and my moon. I will respect you, care for you, and grow with you, through good times and hard times, as your friend, lover, and partner. I once thought you were fragile, like the wings of a butterfly. I was wrong. You are strength and beauty and grace, and I am looking forward to a lifetime of loving you."

His vows in Spanish had me swooning, but hearing him pledge himself to me in front of God, our friends, and family in English has me ready to get him alone so we can seal our vows with our bodies instead of words.

I tamp down the urge and instead recite vows of my own. "How lucky am I to call you mine? Your love for me and trust in me make me a better person daily. You're everything I never knew I needed and fill a void in me I never knew existed. You were there for my darkest moments. You believed in me when I didn't. When I was spiraling out of control, you grounded me. Because of you, I know I am enough. I know I am worthy, wanted, and loved—and I can't wait to make sure you know the same, day in and day out, for the rest of our lives. I love you, Mateo, and I am proud to call you my husband."

After we exchange rings and the officiant prays over us, the moment I've been waiting for is finally here. "By the power vested in me I now pronounce you husband and wife; you may now kiss the bride."

Mateo wraps an arm around my waist, pulls me flush against him, and kisses me like his very existence depends on it. Cupping my cheek with his free hand, he moves his lips against mine in a sensuous dance. This kiss is not only a sealing of our marriage, but a promise of what's to come.

We part—reluctantly—and are introduced as Mr. and Mrs. Reyes. Butterflies fill me at the sound, their wings flapping at warp-speed.

"I love you, Mrs. Reyes," Mateo whispers, clasping his hand in mine for our walk down the aisle as husband and wife.

"What a beautiful ceremony," Letty says, the second we reach the end of the aisle.

"Thank you," I reply, knowing good and well she wanted us to marry in the church.

"It was no St. Peters, but still, very lovely."

Mateo nods, his lips twitching with a barely suppressed smile. "Thank you, Mamá."

"And thank you for allowing us to use your yard," I tack on.

"Of course." My mother-in-law grins. "Now, come, let us celebrate your union."

The next several house pass in a blur of toasts, well wishes, dancing, and mingling, until finally only a few stragglers are left.

I try and help with the cleanup, desperate to get my husband alone so I can give him his wedding gift, but Lety isn't having it.

"You two go; we have this under control," she says, shooing us out the door.

It's on the tip of my tongue to argue, but Mateo doesn't need to be told twice.

I can't help but admire his profile as he drives. He's so insanely handsome—and so totally mine. He takes notice and entwines our hands together and tugs my hand close enough to kiss.

His lips fuel the burning need within me to make this marriage *extra* official.

"Let me check us in," he murmurs, idling the truck in front of the hotel entrance. I fidget the entire time he's gone.

He returns, room key in hand and parks the truck. "Stay put," he commands, causing me to pout.

At my door, he bends and scoops me into his arms. "Mateo," I squeal, throwing my arms around his neck. "You don't have to carry me."

"Yes, I do."

I squirm in his grasp, but he moves steadily ahead, my pleas falling on deaf ears.

He carries me over the threshold of our room—suite actually—stopping only to secure the door before making determined strides to the bed.

Once I'm on my own two feet, he spins me, so my back is to him. He skims his long fingers over my exposed back before nimbly working free the closure.

I love a man with a purpose. And right now, that purpose is getting this dress off as quickly as possible.

I don't know why I'm nervous, but I can't help the little flutters of anticipation running through me. Mateo takes his time, helping me onto the bed before worshiping every inch of skin he reveals until I'm wearing nothing but the special pale blue lingerie I purchased specifically for tonight.

"*Dios mio*," he groans, slowly running his hands up my body. "You are a vision." He leans down to place a gentle kiss on my soft swell of my belly. "And all mine."

I try to sit up, needing to even the clothing score, but he refuses. Instead, I'm gifted with my own private strip show. I'm practically drooling as his suit joins my dress on the floor.

This man is a god. *My* god.

"Is it crazy that I'm nervous?" I ask in a quiet voice.

"Not at all." He hovers above me, careful not to put too much pressure on my stomach. "But this is only the beginning."

Whatever nerves I had disappear in a cloud of lust as he blazes a trail of kisses down my neck, paying special attention to my overly sensitive breasts. I moan under his touch, craving the friction as he rolls his hips, sending a jolt of need directly to my core.

"Tonight, it's only us." He trails his lips even lower, running his hand reverently over my bump. "I can't tell you how much I love seeing you grow with our child."

"Our son," I croak out, hoping this little plan of mine doesn't blow up in my face.

I've been sitting on this information for a few days now, and not telling him was the absolute worst form of torture.

I agonized over the perfect gift to give my him on our wedding night. Then it dawned on me. I could easily take a blood test to find out the sex of our child.

Judging from his glassy eyes and wobbly smile, it was the perfect gift.

"*Un hijo*—a son?" His eyes drop to my stomach again. "You are sure?"

I beam brightly at him as he caresses the space below my naval. "One hundred percent."

Without warning, he straightens his posture and captures my lips with his. This kiss is one fueled by equal parts joy and desire. Mateo makes quick work of removing the remaining lingerie before lining himself up at my entrance.

"I love you, my wife." He enters me slowly.

"I love you too," I cry, as he pulls nearly all the way out of me before slamming back into me in a way that has my back arching while I beg for more.

Mateo plays my body with expertise, knowing exactly where to touch, where to kiss, what spots to hit until I'm practically seeing stars and begging for release.

"Please, Mateo, fuck." He reaches between us to finger my clit, rubbing it in perfect time with his powerful thrusts.

When the first wave hits, I claw at his sweat-slicked back, crying out his name as the orgasm rips through my body.

He reaches down and hikes my right leg over his shoulder. The new position allows him to hit a spot deep within me, which only intensifies the tremors still running through me.

"*Mariposita*," he howls, sounding feral with need. His rhythm falters, and a few unsteady thrusts later, he stills over me, his warm release filling me.

He releases my leg and presses his forehead to mine. He drags precious air into his lungs as our heartbeats slow to a normal level.

"That was…" I can't even finish my sentence because there are no words to describe what we just shared.

"Perfect." Mateo brushes my hair away, giving him an unobstructed view of the smile permanently etched on my face. "It was perfect."

ACKNOWLEDGMENTS

Every single book, I worry I'll forget to thank someone important. It is legit one of my biggest fears, so much so it keeps me up at night.

Because the thing is, writing a book is a lot like raising a child—it takes a village. Thank God, my village is full of the best and brightest. My village is brimming with people I'm simply lucky to know.

So many amazing, kind souls who have gone out of their way to help me, to lend an ear, or a kind word on a down day.

Honestly, there are too many to list.

So, I'll leave it at this:

THANK YOU. YEAH, THAT'S RIGHT…YOU.
FROM THE BOTTOM OF MY HEART, THANK YOU.

I also need to thank my team—Kiezha, Ellie, and Julie, y'all are priceless and I couldn't do this without y'all.

But maybe the most important group I need to thank is the book lovers! Be you a reader or a blogger, you are the reason I am able to do this. Your support means more to me than I'll ever be able to articulate. I am thankful for each and every one of you.

And last but not least, my family. Y'all are my everything and I'm incredibly grateful for the glorious chaos y'all bring. Special shoutout to Baby K—this book almost didn't happen thanks to your special brand of clinginess.

LET'S CONNECT

Known by Kate to most, LK Farlow is an Amazon Top 40 bestselling author of small-town romances.

She has a heart built for happily ever after, which is lucky since she found hers at the young age of nineteen. Now, at thirty, she is the wife to one hunky man and the mother to four human babies and one lizard.

Kate often jokes that her life is all out chaos on most days, but she wouldn't trade it for the world.

Stay in the know with all things LK by subscribing to her newsletter: http://bit.ly/lkfnewsletter

Join her Facebook reader group, LK's Darlings: http://bit.ly/bemydarling

Printed in Great Britain
by Amazon

63089765R00151